FIRE AND GRACE

MELISSA PLANTZ

FIRE and GRACE
Publishing, LLC

Melissa Plantz
FIRE and GRACE Publishing, LLC
fireandgracepublishing.com

Printed in the United States of America
First Printing 2020
First Edition 2020

ISBN: 978-1-7349381-3-5

10 9 8 7 6 5 4 3 2 1

Edited by Roxana Coumans
Cover Design by VC Book Cover Design

To My Family,

With Love

CHAPTER ONE

"I can't believe Iris dropped that bomb on us after all these years. What are we supposed to do now?" My sister, Kory Ann, leaned against the stained-glass window at the front of the funeral home, as she watched the parade of somber guests.

I pressed into her to allow visitors more room to pay their respects. "I don't know, Kory, but it's not like she had a choice. She was dying." I ran a hand through my dark hair, wishing I'd taken the time to curl it this morning instead of entertaining the multitudes of guests bringing food. Most wanted to come inside and chat which made Iris' death that much harder on us.

But, Kory was right.

Iris finally told us the truth about our mother two days before she passed away at the hospice house, losing her battle with breast cancer. It'd been a horrific few months with Iris learning of her Stage IV cancer, and although she tried to fight back with aggressive chemo and radiation, after several weeks of agony, Iris left us.

We made our way up to the casket, sliding around the mourners dressed in their finest. Iris' hands, cold and painted with makeup to hide the bruises from the IVs, now lay lifeless in her lap. She was a shell of her former self with paper thin skin from the chemo and her once beautiful blonde hair replaced by a wig. If only I could see her eyes again. No matter the effects of the treatment, Iris Brewer's eyes always glowed with energy and purpose.

Since Iris had known her diagnosis, she'd made her funeral plans to spare us the stress. She'd preplanned and approved the casket, music, clothes, hair, nails, and makeup. She wore a beautiful dress in a sapphire blue with a matching blue quartz stone necklace she'd crafted. Iris was always making bracelets and necklaces from her treasure hunts on the beach.

After a long while, I noticed that other visitors were waiting to view Iris, their sad smiles directed at us. I glanced at the people – dozens were members from Sweet Hills Baptist, our local church in Locklyn, North Carolina, but many I didn't recognize. I grabbed Kory's hand, and we moved off to the side to greet the mourners and accept their condolences. The next hour went by terribly slow as people filed by, stopping to cry over Iris or hug us way too tightly. I can't stand people pitying me and yet, I felt sorry for us, as well.

Pastor Simms finally appeared at the pulpit and started clearing his throat the same way he did on Sundays to get everyone's attention. The funeral would start any minute. We sat down in the reserved seats for the family on the first row. Sadly, we only needed one row. Iris left so many unanswered questions. What would happen to Kory Ann and me; Kory, at only fifteen, and me, staring down eighteen?

My mind began to wander as the people moved about finding seats. Eight years ago, our mother, unable to care for two little girls, according to Iris because she was a heroin addict, called her aunt Iris one afternoon. After some unfortunate incidents, Iris drove from North Carolina to West Virginia one weekend, placed us in her car, and never looked back. Our mom could have cared less and never even inquired about her daughters. Iris had rarely spoken of Rachel to us, not until she was literally on her deathbed. Never having children of her own, Iris had taken our tangled dark hair and dirty faces in and assumed the motherly role. Our grandparents were long dead and who knew where our father called home. All we knew was that he was Armenian and had at one time attended WVU. Now with Iris lying in a coffin at the end of this meticulous room, we were on our own.

"Did you see the flowers from Mom?" Kory waved her French-manicured hand over towards the casket. I had indeed seen them. All of them. If Rachel was trying to make an impression the impression was rather large. Six huge bouquets flanked the casket with lilies, orchids, and other flowers, and these were just from Rachel and some man named Aiden. Iris' other flowers were minuscule in comparison, including the small bouquet I put together from Iris' own garden.

"At least the flowers are ones she liked, I guess. How did Mom find out she passed anyway? I didn't think Iris talked to her," Kory said.

I waved at my friend Freya and her family who'd just arrived. Freya shot me a look indicating she wanted to come over, but a small group had surrounded her father. He was Mayor of Locklyn and people tended to fawn over their family.

"I don't know. I remember Iris telling us she was our guardian in name only years ago. She never filed legal papers and the school board never asked her about it when she enrolled us in school. You know small town-"

Kory grabbed my hand and squeezed before I could finish, her gaze focused on movement along the wall. I turned as the ache in my belly grew. Kory was not staring at a what, but a whom.

A beautiful woman with long blonde hair and movie star quality style moved along the wall towards the casket followed by a handsome dark-haired man carrying two roses and wearing sunglasses. The woman slowed as she drew closer to the casket. They stopped in front of Iris, and the man removed his sunglasses as he placed his other arm around the woman's shoulders. The whole room hushed including Pastor Simms who no longer cleared his throat for silence. He stared at the couple as well.

The woman lowered her head as if praying and the man whispered something into her ear. She raised a hand to her face and produced a tissue. She wiped her eyes and breathed deeply as the couple turned towards us.

There was no need for introductions. This woman was our mother.

Without a word the woman walked over to me, bent down and kissed my forehead. She did the same to a speechless Kory, who in ordinary circumstances shrank away from people in her personal space but didn't even pull away or turn her head. The woman sat down next to a shocked Kory and crossed her long legs. The man smiled a glistening smile at me, handed each one of us a rose, and sat down beside her.

Kory tightened her grip on my hand as I choked back alarming tears. This had to be the beginning of a nightmare. Surely, I would wake soon.

Rachel had come for her girls.

CHAPTER TWO

The entire funeral was a blur. Pastor Simms delivered the eulogy, and I faintly recalled Kory pulling me along to the limousine provided by the funeral home for the trip to the cemetery. Thankfully, neither Rachel nor the man made any attempts at conversation.

As we sat graveside, Pastor Simms continued the service. Long buried memories dredged up from my subconscious; memories of my mother. A sick feeling threatened to become more than a feeling at any moment.

Rachel certainly did not appear to be a heroin addict or for that matter addicted to anything, except maybe the spa. She was, in a word, perfect. Not a long blonde hair out of place, she had the same cream-colored complexion as Kory and me. Where we both possess dark hair and large, dark almond-shaped eyes, Rachel's eyes, however, were an unsettling sapphire blue. I could almost hear Iris in my head remarking that "the girl smelled of money."

Not that the Brewers did without anything. Iris was neither rich nor poor. She'd invested wisely, believing real wealth wasn't what you made, but what you kept. I never owned a pony, but Iris made sure she paid the bills, food was on the table, and we dressed in the latest trends. Rachel dripped in classic style. Her mere presence demanded respect.

It didn't make sense.

How could a woman whom eight years earlier was in no condition to care for herself let alone her two little girls show up looking like a celebrity from the pages of US Weekly? Not to mention her escort. I had yet to see a man in town who looked anything close to him. The Colin Farrell clone was lean and muscular, dressed conservatively in a close-knit sweater and dress pants. When he smiled, his teeth were perfect. Iris had caps on her teeth, and I wondered if this man did. But, it wasn't just his appearance that made people stare. It was the way he carried himself that matched Rachel.

As the graveside service came to a close, Kory pressed into my shoulder with her chin. "I want to stay while they lower her casket."

"We are. I already told Pastor Simms we would take the limo back and he said it'd take us directly to the house," I whispered back. Kory nodded her head. As if on cue, Rachel's guest sitting behind us leaned in between our heads. His breath smelled of cinnamon.

"Girls, your mother and I are going to stop by your aunt's house after the service. The four of us need to talk about some things," he said in an Irish accent. I watched as Kory nodded her head at him. The gesture seemed to make him happy, and he sat back in his chair. I sat motionlessly. I would need to talk to Kory alone in the limo before we arrived at the house. We didn't even know these people. Rachel was merely a memory, and maybe not even that for Kory.

It was my job now to protect my sister. Something inside nagged at me. And it wasn't just Iris' death.

As we stood up to leave the graveside, Pastor Simms approached us. "Girls, again, I am so very sorry for your loss of Iris." He gave both of us quick hugs.

"Thank you, Pastor Simms. The service was beautiful," Kory said, and I nodded in agreement.

"You do plan to let the driver take you home, right?"

"Yes, sir," I said as I glanced across the cemetery at the limo waiting under an old oak tree. The graveyard belonged to Sweet Hills Baptist Church and was part of its acreage. I couldn't see the church building from here, but the recreation building stood right outside the gates.

"Pastor Simms?" Rachel placed a hand on the preacher's arm. "My name is Rachel Brewer, Iris's niece. Thank you for the service. It was wonderful."

Pastor Simms turned and greeted our mother like a long, lost friend. "Rachel Brewer! I can't tell you how happy I am to meet you finally. Iris told me you would come. And I must say you are beautiful, despite the circumstances."

"Thank you," Rachel said, whipping her blown-out locks to the right. "This is my fiancé, Aiden Blake." The two men shook hands and Aiden said something quietly to Pastor Simms which caused the tall, southern man to laugh heartily.

The two men continued to talk as I turned on my heel and made my way through the mourners to the awaiting limo when Freya stopped me.

Never one to care about other people's personal spaces, she pulled me into a tight hug. After she doled one out to my sister, Kory waved to a friend and went to join him.

"I'm sooo sorry, Ava," Freya said, giving the word 'so' its own area code. Unlike my sister, I didn't make friends quite as easily. I'd met Freya in the sixth grade, and we'd decided right then to be friends until death do us part. Her blonde ponytail and perky nature was the perfect contrast to my serious, and somewhat, sarcastic nature.

Freya motioned towards the couple with Pastor Simms. "Oh, girl! Is that your mother?" She was one of the very few people that knew the real reason why we lived with Iris and not our mother.

"Apparently so," I said. "They're coming over to the house."

Freya regarded the happy couple now busy greeting other mourners. "Well, she's gorgeous. And I could stare at him all day."

"Freya," I said.

Freya whipped her blonde ponytail around as she faced me. "Okay, okay. I know this can't be easy on you. Her turning up today of all days. Try to get some rest. I'll call you tonight." She gave me a quick hug before she went to find her parents.

No, not easy at all.

~ ~ ~

"Who is that guy anyway?" I'd wailed about Rachel and her man in a hushed tone since we'd left the cemetery as I didn't want the driver from the funeral home to hear.

Kory let out an exasperated sigh.

"Kory, I don't know what they want, but I have a gut feeling it's about parental rights."

She stared at her hands resting in her lap. "You think Mom is here to take over? Maybe to move in with us at Iris' house?" She rolled her eyes. "After eight years of not a word? Don't overreact, Ava. I mean, did you see her? There is no way she is on drugs. Do you think that guy is her husband?"

"Overreact? Kory, Rachel shows up here out of nowhere on the day of Iris' funeral to pay her respects after years, and then leave? I don't think so. She wants something and her husband, or whatever, is right along with her. Look, no matter what, keep calm. We see the lawyer next week, and there is no way Iris left us to fend for ourselves in the hands of that woman."

"I'm the only one calm, Ava." Kory rolled her eyes again and looked out the window.

I sank back into the plush leather seat. I felt the years of anger and bitterness rage inside of me. Part of me knew what Iris said about Rachel was true. What kind of mother could give away her children and never have a second thought about them? As the limo pulled around the corner of the dead-end street, I could see a sleek black Lincoln with West Virginia tags parked in front of the house.

They were already here.

CHAPTER THREE

I put on a pot of coffee while Kory sliced pineapple upside down cake, made by one of the church ladies, for our unwanted guests. Rachel Brewer and Aiden Blake, as Rachel had introduced him on the porch, were making themselves comfortable in the living room. We could hear Rachel reminiscing about the house, regaling stories of her childhood and Aunt Iris. Her laughter was familiar as a memory tried to flood my mind, but I managed to push it as far back as I could while pouring the creamer into the little serving pitcher.

After arranging the slices of cake on a platter and gathering saucers and forks, Kory waited for me to finish collecting everything for the coffee. Iris owned so many serving pieces because she believed you should always offer guests food and coffee no matter how many times they visited your home. I couldn't help but allow my hand to linger a little longer over the china sugar bowl with the rose motif – Iris' favorite piece. Kory wrapped her arms around my shoulders. The two of us stood in front of the kitchen window like that for a long while until the coffeemaker beeped. I managed to balance the tray with the carafe, creamer, sugar, spoons, and mugs into the living room with Kory behind me carrying the slices of cake.

Rachel and Aiden stopped talking as we entered the room and watched us place everything on the coffee table. I sat down in Iris' favorite rocker as Kory started handing out the little saucers of cake. Aiden took the initiative to serve coffee. I noticed he didn't ask Rachel how she wanted her coffee. He handed the cup to her, and she thanked him. Obviously, they knew each other very well.

When everyone had their coffee and cake, Aiden spoke first. "Rachel was telling me what a wonderful and caring person your great aunt was. I am sorry for your loss."

"Thank you," Kory half whispered, sipping her coffee.

After a few moments of awkward silence, Rachel turned to me. "It really is good to see you and Kory after all these years. You both have turned into beautiful young women. I'm sorry it took something like this to bring me to you. I wish I'd known Iris was sick sooner."

"How did you know at all? We didn't think you had any contact with us here." My inner demons threatened a full onslaught war, and I bit my lower lip, afraid they may break free. Iris hated rudeness, but with so much resentment built up, I didn't know if I could hold it all in and remain civil.

Rachel tilted her head, and a sad smile crossed her face. "Iris called me two weeks ago and told me about her aggressive breast cancer. She said she knew I was much better off than before and it was time the two of you came back home to West Virginia."

I stared at Rachel in stunned silence, mid-sip. Iris had known how to reach Rachel and called her? Kory and I exchanged glances. With a mouth full of pineapple-upside down cake, she raised one eyebrow to urge me to say something, do something, and if I didn't, she definitely would. Iris always got onto Kory about her sarcastic, edgy nature that sometimes bordered on the unladylike.

I took a deep breath measuring out my words in case Rachel did fry all of her brain cells once upon a time. "You're saying Iris called you because she was dying? No offense, but why would she do that? We haven't seen or heard from you in eight years. You don't know anything about us. And as for moving back to West Virginia, I don't think so. We have an appointment next week with the lawyer regarding the will. I only have one more year of school, and I'll be eighteen next week. I can make sure Kory finishes high school here. This is our home." I set my coffee cup down a little too hard on the table.

Aiden handed his mug to Rachel and picked up his cell phone. The blonde Aphrodite posing as our mother smiled again, a patient if not somewhat patronizing smile. She reached into her handbag and pulled out a stack of photos.

I recognized the pictures as I flipped through each one. Kory came over for a closer look and sat on the arm of the rocker to stop it from moving. These were pictures from grade school graduation, middle school graduation, our first bikes, Christmases, Easters, baptisms, school plays, dance recitals, my softball games; every milestone from our childhood summed up in this stack.

"Iris has been sending me pictures and letters since I got my act together. I've been clean for four years. It wasn't that hard to find me, thanks to Aiden," Rachel said.

I glanced at the man talking on his cell phone quietly in the hallway. I handed the pictures to Kory.

"What do you mean it wasn't hard to find you?" Kory asked Rachel while thumbing back through the pictures.

"Well, because of my addiction to several drugs, my life hit rock bottom. I was contemplating suicide when Aiden walked into my life and showed me there is a better way." She looked longingly into the hallway at the source of her change.

"So, what, you found God?" Kory asked. She'd taken her dark hair down from the clip, the massive amount framed her face and gave her a wild appearance.

"Kind of," Rachel answered in a conspirator's tone. "Aiden is the head of a group called the Order of Greatness. Once I found it, I found the true me and what I am meant to do in life. It changed everything for me." Rachel could barely contain her excitement. I turned to Kory who leaned in to catch every word. The sick feeling returned to my stomach.

Rachel, continued, "The Order believes you can heal yourself from your past and your physical ailments by focusing on your inner power. They believe everyone, and everything is connected. In my case, overcoming my drug addiction meant facing certain truths about myself and my past and learning to let go. I have so much to share with you." She smiled as she shrugged her shoulders as if she were on the verge of spilling secrets to her sorority sisters.

Aiden returned to the living room, a charming smile on his face as he poured himself more coffee. "I just got off the phone with William Michaels, your aunt's solicitor."

I looked him square in the eye. "I know who Mr. Michaels is. We don't know who you are in all of this."

The smile never left his face. "I am your mother's fiancé, your soon-to-be stepfather. As I was saying, all of us now have an appointment with Mr. Michaels tomorrow morning at nine. After the reading of the will, we will need to go to the courthouse and see Judge Hemsworth for the final approval."

Rachel smiled all over herself. "Perfect. Problem solved. By the end of next week, you two can be at home with us. You are going to love the house. It is five times larger than this one. It's called the Carey House, and it's where the Order meets. It has historical significance. You'll see what I mean when you get there."

"We're not supposed to see Mr. Michaels until the end of next week," Kory said in a small voice.

My anger hit its boiling point. How this man had been able to make changes to the lawyer's appointment and arrange a meeting with a judge in a matter of minutes was beyond me.

"I think you two should leave now. Kory and I have had a very long and stressful day." I kept my eyes locked on Aiden. He drank down his mug of coffee in one large swig.

"I believe Ava is right, Rachel. We had better let the girls rest before tomorrow. We'll meet you two at Mr. Michaels' office, or do you need a ride?" Aiden asked as he stood to leave. Rachel picked up her handbag and took the photos from Kory. My little sister didn't respond. She was staring straight ahead at the coffee table.

"I have my license. I'll drive Iris' car in the morning," I said.

"Great. Then we will meet you at nine." And with that, he and Rachel went out the front door. Neither of us walked them to the door, and I had the amusing thought that Iris would have found that disrespectful. You should always see your guests out the door.

But Iris wasn't here anymore.

~ ~ ~

As we washed the few dishes dirtied and straightened the kitchen, the conversation focused on our new upside-down lives.

"What I'm saying is I feel the same way you do about Mom, Ava." Kory dried a plate and placed it in the cabinet above her head. "But how else could she have those pictures of us unless Iris sent them to her? Iris knew she was dying and thought having Mom in our lives was best."

"That doesn't make it the best decision. You know Iris was on a lot of painkillers toward the end. She probably wasn't thinking straight the day she called Rachel." I still refused to call that woman Mom. I washed and rinsed a glass and stuck it into the drain for Kory. "And anyway, who are these people? You heard what she said. She only came clean after meeting him and some Order of Greatness, or something. She all but said she belonged to a cult, Kory."

Kory put down the glass she was drying. "Really? A cult? I think you're reaching now. I know you have reservations about Mom and Aiden, but this is our chance, Ava. Truth is she is still our Mom. Iris called her because she was worried about us and this guy is going to be our stepfather. Our chance to have parents, a real family, is now. Something we've never had. If it means moving to a state I don't remember, then that's fine with me."

"And leaving your friends and everything you've ever known?"

She shrugged, "I can always FaceTime them and I'll come back and visit when I can. Plus, there's nothing stopping me from having my friends visit me. This might actually be a good thing for you. Force you to make new friends."

I took a deep breath and ignored her last comment. Kory's longing to be part of a traditional family blinded her from sensing the danger ahead that I could feel in my bones.

"I'm calling it a night." I let the soapy water out of the sink. "I'm going to get in my yoga practice and then soak in the tub. We need to leave around eight-forty in the morning."

Kory didn't turn around but kept placing the newly dried glasses into the cabinet. "Kory, look at me. Please." I stood against the doorway leading to the dining room. I could see the strain on her face. This had been a rough day for her too. "You're my little sister. I'll do whatever is best for you, for both of us. What's meant to happen will happen."

Kory mustered a bittersweet smile. I headed to my room and tried to push the thoughts of Rachel and Aiden out of my head.

After twenty minutes of yoga practice, I felt a little less stressed, but couldn't bring myself to call Freya. Her bubbly personality was too much for the occasion. As the bathtub filled with water, I tossed in a bath bomb and watched it fizz. The coconut-scented ball sent bubbles into the water and the smell was divine. I eased into the tub and laid back. There had to be a way to deal with Rachel and her fiancé without losing our right to stay in the house.

I closed my eyes and breathed in the water's beach scent. My body relaxed as I began to slip into sleep. Disjointed images shot through my dreams. A medieval church. An angel with large dark wings. Iris threw something blue and shiny to me as she said something - something urgent - but I couldn't quite catch it.

The final image was of Rachel, her arms soaked in blood, mouthing the words, "help me."

I jerked awake.

CHAPTER FOUR

The next morning, we appeared at William Michaels' office dressed in our Sunday best. I wore a gray A-skirt with a ruffle at the slit and a white ruffle blouse open above the center allowing a silver camisole to show with beads of varying lengths around my neck. I'd seen an actress on a court show wear a similar outfit and decided today was the perfect day to try it out. Kory dressed simple in an emerald green sheath dress and matching wedges with a little white jacket. Iris would be proud. We needed Mr. Michaels to take us seriously and hoped there was a way we could stay on our own at the house. At least that was my prayer.

Rachel and Aiden were in the waiting area when we arrived talking to Kory's friend, Dillon. Dillon's mother had worked for Mr. Michaels for as long as I could remember.

"Hey, Kory! What up, A?" Dillon smiled when he saw my sister. His two-year crush on her was embarrassing. I smiled back at him as Kory gave him a hug. "Sorry about Iris," he said, and I could tell he was genuinely moved. Iris was always nice to our friends although Dillon sometimes tried her patience. It's not that he was a bad kid by any means. He was just high-strung. Iris had told Dillon once that he could run a train ragged and she had no idea how his parents kept up with him. The boy had simply taken off his ever-present ball cap and laughed.

Dillon's mother, Mrs. Petry, came out of the lawyer's personal office and motioned for him to go as we had an appointment with Mr. Michaels this morning.

"I'm going, Mom," Dillon said as he hugged my sister for the second time. "Bye, A," he said to me before he turned back to Kory. "I'll call you later." I forfeited the opportunity to roll my eyes in response to Dillon's apparent Kory-crush as I had a bigger problem today.

After he left, Aiden greeted us with that charming smile. Rachel went so far as to hug us, and I couldn't help but notice Kory neither pulled away nor hugged back.

William Michaels was an old friend of Iris' and she trusted him totally with matters both legal and financial. He'd been to the house on many occasions throughout the years, but today I needed him to see us as young adults and not children. Mr. Michaels was a large man with small glasses who always wore a suit no matter the temperature outside. I asked Iris many years ago why Mr. Michaels always wore the same suit and smelled of sweat. Iris told me matter of fact, "We do not make fun of people, Ava. We treat everyone with respect and help everyone we can." The next Christmas Iris gave three new suits to Mr. Michaels.

When Mr. Michaels opened the door to his inner office and came out, he shook his head and hugged me tightly, swallowing me in a bear hug, and then patted Kory on the shoulder. He knew of her dislike of hugs from non-school friends. He introduced himself to Rachel and Aiden.

Aiden displayed his magnetism and charisma and within a few minutes the two men were talking and laughing like frat brothers. I had to give Aiden credit. He had the ability to make people feel special as if his sole focus was on that one individual. Rachel stood beside Aiden with a proud smile on her face. He wore gray dress pants and a dark blue button down untucked tailored shirt that fit him perfectly while she looked more like The First Lady than a grieving woman here to listen to the reading of a will. She wore a conservative powder blue suit with a single strand of pearls around her neck.

"Please, please, come inside and sit down. Iris was a good friend of mine and we want to get through these legalities as easily as possible." Mr. Michaels motioned us inside and pointed to the dark wood chairs surrounding the old walnut table. Kory and I sat on one side of the massive table and Rachel and Aiden sat across from us. Aiden grinned at me as the sick feeling returned to my stomach. It wasn't the grin; it was the look out of his eyes that left me a bit disturbed, although I couldn't put my finger on why.

After a grueling twenty minutes, it seemed Kory and I were nodding off from the stress and legal terminology. Mr. Michaels was trying to explain the will to us, but it also seemed as if he were accommodating Aiden and Rachel in the meeting.

"I really don't understand what any of this has to do with us. I mean we are going to get to stay at the house, right?" I didn't want to mince words with Mr. Michaels especially with Aiden and Rachel sitting there.

"Yes, right, yes, Ava, I am trying to get to that."

Mr. Michaels shifted in his chair. He seemed hesitant to explain it. Nervous is a better word. His eyes darted towards Aiden. Ever since Aiden entered our lives, the last twenty-four hours consisted of people wanting to please him inexplicably. Did Kory notice?

"Ava, I think that if you'll just be patient, Mr. Michaels is trying to explain to you and Kory exactly what your great aunt Iris has left you and what her wishes were. Iris seems to have been a very intelligent woman, and a responsible woman at that. She only wanted what was best for the two of you meaning that you come to live with Rachel at her home in West Virginia and leave North Carolina…at least until you finish high school."

Aiden leaned across the table as he squeezed Rachel's hand. I couldn't believe this man had the audacity to sit here and explain these things to us, this perfect stranger. Kory didn't meet my gaze. She stared at him open-mouthed.

"That can't possibly be right. This has been our home for eight years." I glared at Mr. Michaels and Aiden. "Iris would've never moved us back to West Virginia with both of us still in school. There's no way. I am more than capable of taking care of Kory while she finishes school. Mr. Michaels, how can this be happening? I mean is that even legal? We've not lived with our mother in eight years and Iris raised us. Can you honestly expect us to move to another state to live with a woman we don't even know? No offense, Rachel."

Part of me felt bad for Rachel having said what I did, but what she was doing wasn't okay, that going to live with her didn't fix anything nor did it redeem her of the mistakes she made in the past. My job now, my responsibility, was to my sister.

Mr. Michaels was sweating now. He shifted a little bit more in his chair and I could tell he was very uncomfortable with this entire situation. Rachel didn't say a word after my outburst, but sat observing the showdown between Mr. Michaels, Aiden, and me. Poor Kory sat mute staring down at the table.

Aiden wore a look of fascination, apparently surprised by my challenging him. I had the feeling he didn't meet many people who dared to question him, let alone defy him.

Mr. Michaels finally found his voice. "Ava, please, I know you're upset and all of this has been a real shock to you and Kory and in that I am deeply, deeply sorry. You know what a good friend Iris was to me and the Brewers have always been a wonderful family here in town. Now you'll be eighteen next week and by law, although you do have one more year of school, you can stay here and live in the house. There is more than enough money in the trust to take care of you and to pay the bills. Iris' portfolio is widely diversified with investments, ETFs, real estate, and even gold. And I know you are a responsible young lady and would be fine. However, Kory is only fifteen. She has to live with a legal guardian and that cannot be you."

Mr. Michaels bowed his head before continuing, "That only leaves your mother, Rachel Brewer. Now unless Rachel would like to move to North Carolina, which I don't believe she does," Mr. Michaels glanced quickly over to Rachel and Aiden, then back to me, "then Kory will have to move to West Virginia, at least until she finishes school which is still two more years. So, I suppose the real question is do you think you could move to West Virginia to be with Kory for these next two years, or do you want to stay here by yourself?"

Deep inside, I said a prayer to God. How could this be happening to us? Separated from Kory? That was impossible. Mr. Michaels already knew that. More than likely Kory knew my answer. Although there were times I wanted to choke her, I would never leave my sister even if our mother and her new friend were not the people raising her.

Iris used to say that sometimes in life you must make hard decisions, decisions you wouldn't normally make. So, then the question becomes, do you choose the solution that is safe and comfortable for you, or do you do the thing that scares you the most to protect the ones you love? I knew that Kory wanted to have a family; a traditional family, with a mother and father and sister, but our mother Rachel and our soon-to-be stepfather Aiden did not fit the mold of the traditional family. Did she not have the same sensation of evil, the feeling of urgency I did every time I looked at them? How could she not be aware of it?

Kory's face said it all. She needed me to stay with her, to protect her from what may lie ahead, and to help her finish school. It was the responsible thing to do.

"If that's our only option for Kory to move to West Virginia to finish high school while living with Rachel and Aiden, then I'll go with her, Mr. Michaels. She's my sister and we're family," I looked directly at Rachel. "And a real family sticks together no matter what happens."

~ ~ ~

The rest of the morning flew by. When we finished the meeting with Mr. Michaels, he took us to meet with the judge. The judge read over the will to make it official, stating that Kory must go with Rachel to West

Virginia, and dividing the trust with me acting as beneficiary when I turned eighteen next week. In the meantime, Mr. Michaels would assume the role as beneficiary.

Kory never said much of anything the whole morning, but I could tell she was partly devastated, her dry, sarcastic nature hidden well. We were leaving our friends and our routines and everything from our childhood, yet I knew that secretly my sister wanted this family ideal. Aiden informed us he would send movers to the house next week to help us box what we wanted to take. Of course, the house would remain empty and he would arrange for a caretaker to make sure no one broke in. Rachel thought it would be a great idea for us to take vacations back here to visit our friends and the nearby beach.

We agreed that after I finished high school I would move back and live in the house. That was the only bright part of the day. Finally, after much discussion, Aiden and Rachel agreed to allow Kory and me to stay at the house alone the following week to pack. He would call and let us know what day to expect the movers and we explained to him we would probably only have a few heavy boxes.

Rachel went on and on about the large Carey House, our soon-to-be new home. Lyle Carey apparently founded the Order of Greatness and built the house to his specifications to facilitate meetings. Rachel said she would spend this week readying up our bedrooms. She said we each would have our own large room.

Not that I believed her. She would probably say anything to get us to stay with her. All I wanted to do was to get rid of them, to send Rachel and Aiden back to West Virginia, and finally sit down and talk about this bizarre day with Kory.

After they finally left in their sleek black car, I fixed myself an iced coffee to relax and stretched out on the chaise on the back porch underneath the trees to stare up at the porch ceiling fans as they created the only breeze on this hot summer day. Kory was in her room. I could talk to her in a bit.

Our entire world was shaken to its core.

I needed some peace and to know it was going to be okay because I felt like a war was coming.

I slapped a mosquito trying to feast on my thigh, its blood smearing across my leg as I pressed the call button on Freya's picture on my phone. She answered on the second ring and I filled her in on the last two days. She sounded shocked and appalled that Rachel and Aiden had swooped in and enacted parental rights on Kory, thus forcing me to move too. We talked for about an hour before I told her I needed a nap.

I couldn't put my finger on it, but there was something so charming about Aiden – and so otherworldly – something dangerous under his skin. I wondered what last night's dream meant, if anything. I'd only seen flashes, but the angel with the dark wings in my dream looked vaguely familiar. But, wasn't that the purpose of dreams? Weren't they supposed to help your mind process events from the real world? If that was true, then who was the man and why was Rachel bleeding and asking for help?

And what was Iris trying to tell me?

CHAPTER FIVE

The next couple of days were disorienting at best. I'd gone down to the local grocery store to pick up a few boxes we could use to pack. Kory and I would talk about our memories of Iris and the fun things we did in the house and out in the garden. We both cried and talked about our fears and what this new change might mean for us. Kory had high hopes for our new life with Rachel and Aiden. I wasn't convinced that this move was the best thing, but I didn't have a choice. Not really. Eventually, word got out about town that Kory and I were moving, and friends came to visit us.

One evening after a run to the store, I came home to find three girls hanging out on the front porch with Kory.

"Hey," I said to them as I carried an armload of grocery bags up the steps. None of the girls raced down to help me. A redhaired girl half-waved in my direction.

"Hi! We just stopped by to see if Kory needed help packing."

"I told them we're almost done, but Lydia insisted on ordering pizza. We're waiting on it now," Kory said as she pushed herself on the porch swing.

"Thank you, Lydia. That's very nice of you," I said, and suddenly knew how Iris must have felt when she'd come home and find random kids on her porch. I still wasn't sure which girl was Lydia. Kory made friends easily and had never met a stranger. I stopped at the front door.

"Kory, why won't you come help me put these away?"

"Not now. We're waiting on the pizza."

"I need your help," I said, a bit more sternly.

"Help with what? Putting away popsicles? I think you can handle it." The girls laughed at Kory's sarcasm. I went inside and slammed the door. Maybe everyone was right. Maybe I couldn't raise Kory for the next two years. I was her sister, not her mother or her great-aunt. I could count on her to remain respectful in front of adults, the way Iris raised us, but in front of her friends? She was the edgy, take-no-crap-from-her-peers Brewer girl.

Kory's friends weren't the only ones to stop by and visit, thank God. The neighbors across the street, Dillon's mother, Freya, and Pastor Simms all took the time to spend a couple of hours with us.

I'd always liked Pastor Simms. He had a slight Southern accent with a deep voice that made you pay attention during church services. Not to mention, he was a good six feet and five inches tall, if not taller.

When he stopped by the house one afternoon, I invited him into the living room to talk. I wanted his take on our situation with Rachel and Aiden and maybe have him say a prayer for us.

Kory confronted me in the kitchen as I made some coffee for our guest. We still had an abundance of food from the continuous visits from friends and our church family.

"Seriously, Ava? You're being paranoid. I know you're asking Pastor Simms to stay because you want to talk to him about this conspiracy you think Rachel and Aiden are involved in. Why can't you leave it alone? Things are not going to be as bad as you keep making them. It's a change and you need to get over it." Kory jerked the refrigerator door open.

"No, you need to wake up. I don't have a good feeling about this and I don't know why you don't feel the same way. Have you not felt anything weird when Aiden is around or when Rachel talks about this slimy Order of Greatness?"

I started washing out the coffee pot as Kory pulled the strawberry pretzel salad out of the refrigerator and cut a large piece for Pastor Simms who was still waiting patiently in the living room.

"Just stop it, Ava."

"You want Rachel and Aiden to be the perfect parents," I said in a hushed tone. "What you're being is a try-hard. They're not perfect and don't even count as parents. I'll never forgive Rachel for giving us away." I flipped on the coffeemaker, my hand shaking from wanting to yell and trying to stay quiet at the same time.

Kory turned to glare at me, her brown eyes matching mine, but hers looked almost amber from the fire burning inside of her. Very rarely have I ever seen Kory so angry, let alone, angry at me.

"You girls need any help?" Pastor Simms's voice boomed through the house.

"No, we're almost done. We'll be right there." Kory shook her head at me.

I quickly finished getting coffee for the three of us. It was a few minutes later before Kory announced after she served Pastor Simms his dessert, she was going out to the garden. She didn't want to be a part of me airing dirty laundry about our family as if Pastor Simms didn't already know about why Iris raised us. I found it best just to roll my eyes and stay quiet.

Fifteen minutes later Pastor Simms and I were in deep discussion on the living room sofa about this Order of Greatness. He agreed with me it sounded like the possibility of a cult to him as well and he was quite concerned about Kory and me. I told him I didn't know what to think about the situation and how I should handle things with Kory. I knew Iris would hate the idea of us becoming involved with such a group. He suggested that, if there was any truth to my fears, these types of gatherings tended to draw demonic forces and with Kory at an age of influence this all worried him greatly. He said he didn't get any bad vibes from Rachel and Aiden when he met them, but then again, neither had mentioned leading such an organization.

As we were talking, I began to feel strange. It started deep within me, a vibration, and I looked about the room to see if anything else moved. It felt as if someone reached into my soul and shook me very hard. I looked at Pastor Simms as I struggled not to black out, but he didn't notice anything. The quaking inside grew and I leaned back against the sofa. I watched as the plates and cups on the coffee table vibrated constantly as the whole room shook. I pulled my legs up against my chest and heard Pastor Simms say, "Ava! What's wrong, girl?"

That's when I saw it. Huddled over in the corner, a man with his back to me, crouched. I opened my mouth, but no sound came out while my heart pounded, and the strawberry pretzel salad moved its way up into my throat.

I stared at the man - not a man – with tunnel vision, nothing else in the room existed. And I knew, just knew he was going to look at me. About the time the thought crossed my mind he turned. His face contorted as his hollow black eyes seeped black sludge down his face. Then everything went black.

~ ~ ~

Kory was leaning over me on the couch when I came to. Pastor Simms handed me a glass of water as Kory helped me to sit up. I kept asking where the man-thing had gone. "What man, Ava?" She asked, frowning.

"Did I black out? I saw a man, something, over in the corner before everything went black." I pointed over to the now empty corner of the room. Pastor Simms and Kory exchanged glances with each other. Their eyes fell back on me.

"Ava dear, there's no one here but us. You blacked out. Do you think maybe you got too hot? You were getting excited about the topic of our conversation." Pastor Simms wore a concerned look on his face but smiled. I sat up a little more and shook my head.

I knew what I'd seen. And I still couldn't shake the feeling there was more to come. Although the thing had said nothing out loud, a voice had penetrated my mind before everything went dark.

He's going to take them all to Hell.

CHAPTER SIX

Exactly one week after Aiden and Rachel left Locklyn, a large moving truck pulled up in front of our home. It appeared out of place in front of the meticulous yard; a rather large, ugly, orange and white truck in front of the little yellow and white house with flowers across the front windowsills and down the sidewalks.

Kory and I sat on the front porch swing resting from a full day of packing boxes. We'd hired Dillon to mow and trim the yard to keep it to Iris' standards and he'd left only a few minutes earlier. He'd thought it was awful that we had to move away and demanded we let him talk to Aiden. It took several minutes of prodding to get him to realize that this was a court order, and nothing could change it. At least for now.

We'd told Aiden we wouldn't need a large moving truck since we didn't have that much to take, however after sorting through Iris' things we found there were quite a few items we wanted with us in West Virginia. Along with paperwork and important legal documents, there was quite a few expensive glassware pieces passed down throughout our family. Instead of leaving it in the house to take a chance on something stolen, even with a caretaker hired by Aiden, Kory and I decided to take most of the breakables with us except for the dishes. We were also taking all of our clothes and almost everything in our bedrooms except for the furniture. Reading was one of my favorite hobbies, so I had at least two boxes full of books. And when it came to clothing, Kory probably had five boxes for every one of mine.

We watched as two men and a woman climbed out of the cab of the box truck. The older man looked to be in his fifties with white hair and a lean build that indicated he was active and fit.

There was a good-looking boy with him, maybe a couple of years older than me with blond hair. Actually, he was to die-for and I glanced at Kory to get her reaction, but she was staring at the woman with an amused smile.

The woman seemed to be about the same age as the man with the exception that her hair was dark and as she approached me I noticed she had a little bit of white hair appearing at the temples. She smiled so wide, it threatened to swallow her face.

"Hi, you girls must be Ava Grace and Kory Ann. Aiden and Rachel have told us so much about you. My name is Julia Carter, and this is my husband, Roger. And this young man is Jake Henderson." The man and woman smiled, and Jake gave me and Kory a once over glance. I knew boys like him at school, preppy boys with expensive clothes and trendy hair. Jake fit all the criteria wearing an outfit I'd probably seen in a Buckle store window display. Those were the ones that usually only looked at a girl for one thing.

I at once disliked him.

Kory got up from the swing and walked casually over to the entrance to the porch. "So, Aiden sent you to help us get these boxes moved? Let me get you some iced tea. We made some this morning."

"Oh, that would be magnificent. The drive here in that thing seemed to take so long. Not to mention cramped. But, Aiden said the sooner he got you moved, the sooner you could be with your mother. She is such a beautiful and sweet woman. We just love her!" the woman said, a little too exuberantly. I didn't move from the swing. It's not that I wanted to be rude to these people. It wasn't their fault that everything had changed in my life the last couple of weeks. I thanked God that school was out for now so at least we didn't have to deal with classes in the middle of all this.

Julia and Roger stepped up onto the porch and I motioned for them to both sit. Iris kept a porch full of rockers. Jake stood on the sidewalk with one foot on the bottom step.

Although I didn't want to be the sweet and generous person, I am. I moved over a bit on the swing and graciously motioned for him to sit with me. "Here, Jake, there's no reason to stand. It'll be soon enough that we'll get to moving those boxes into the truck." He nodded his head, almost sheepishly. And for a second, I wondered if I misjudged him.

Kory came out of the house with the pitcher of iced tea on a tray with glasses of ice and set them on the small table.

Julia looked a little shocked. "Well, you girls are certainly very mature for your age. Rachel said you are seventeen, is that right?" Her eyes landed on me as she took a long sip of her iced tea.

"I'll be eighteen tomorrow and a Senior this Fall. Kory will be a Junior. She's fifteen."

Kory sat down in the rocker at the other end of the porch and scooted in a little closer. She wore a goofy smile on her face that I knew she reserved for whenever a cute boy was around. She rolled her large dark eyes over towards Jake. "Jake, how old are you?"

Jake was reaching for his iced tea, caught off guard by Kory's question he almost knocked over the glass. "I'll be nineteen in October."

Kory was a little disappointed with this news. That would make this boy four years older than she was and in her world that was a little too old. I smiled. As if reading my mind, Kory shot me a look and then got up and poured herself another glass of iced tea.

Julia decided to continue with the conversation while the had-yet-to-say-a-word Roger drank his tea. "But the two of you must be very mature to stay in this house by yourselves since your aunt passed away. I know lots of teenagers you could never trust to do so. Or at least, you can't leave them alone for such a long period of time and still have a house standing. What, with parties and people stopping by. I half-expected to drive up and see a house full of kids!"

I tried to envision what Julia must've expected. "A house full of teens complete with a party, beer, and pizza?" I laughed, and Kory joined in, but she was the only one. It seemed Julia and Roger took me a little too seriously. Of course, this may have fit if they'd pulled up a few days ago when Kory's friends were here eating pizza and drinking Dr. Pepper on the front porch. I looked over at Jake to see if he was in fact a Stepford son in the Order of Greatness. He wore a little bit of a smirk on his face. I couldn't tell if the smirk was him making fun of me or if he enjoyed my comment.

Julia opened her mouth as if to say more, but Roger decided it was time for us all to get to work.

Two hours later, everything that was important to Kory and me was on a moving truck on its way to West Virginia with the three people from the Order of Greatness we'd just met. As we sat on the front steps watching the truck turnaround in the loop of the dead-end street, I felt the now all too familiar sadness. Every step in this new adventure didn't seem right to me. Our lives were changing so fast and I had no way to control it.

Kory got up from the steps. "Hey, I'm going to head on in, get a shower, and wash this crud off me. Mom's supposed to be here in the morning to pick us up and I want to make sure I have my bag packed. I'm afraid I'll forget something." Instead, she stood there for a moment, leaning against the banister.

When I nodded my head as an answer, she went on into the house, shutting the screen door behind her. I sat there a while longer staring at the houses around me, the flowers, the bird bath, and the other yard fixtures. I wanted to memorize everything exactly the way it was, the way it had always been.

Memorizing the yard wouldn't change anything. I couldn't bring Iris back from the dead. Yet all of this wouldn't be so bad if Rachel had always been a part of our lives and I didn't feel dread when I looked at Aiden. After that visit from the thing, hallucination or not, I just didn't know how long I could stay in West Virginia with these people. Pastor Simms chalked up my apparent hallucination as one of three things, quite possibly the combination of all three: overheating, grief, or stress and anxiety.

I did have to admit I was a little curious about this Order of Greatness. Roger, Julia, and Jake were all members and seemed normal. I wondered if my stressed-out subconscious would cause me to hallucinate more creatures the closer we came to whatever this group was. Anytime I approached the subject, Kory shut me down. I didn't blame her. She wanted to have a normal life with a real family and here I was trying to discuss invisible creatures.

I decided the best thing to do was to get out my journal and write before bed. This was something I'd been doing a long time, since my seventh grade English teacher encouraged us to keep one that entire school year. It helped me to figure things out and sometimes see things in the big picture. Iris had called it a diary one time and I hurriedly corrected her. I told her no, it was a book, a book of my day-to-day life. I told her maybe one day I would publish my journals as a memoir. She smiled a knowing smile and told me that my destiny included great things, but if I wanted to keep a *diary* I could.

The memories of Iris again filled me with sadness and I went on in the house to get things ready for tomorrow's trip, locking the door behind me. Rachel would be here in the morning.

CHAPTER SEVEN

The next day, the trip to West Virginia took around eight hours. Rachel arrived at five o'clock in the morning and after we served her a small breakfast and cleaned up the kitchen, the three of us set out in her car with our bags in the trunk. The car was spacious inside and still had that new car smell attached to it. I didn't ask if the car belonged to her or Aiden. Probably the latter.

Around 11 o'clock we stopped at a rest stop and about an hour later stopped for lunch. The conversation in the car was a little strange with Rachel doing most of the talking. She came off as nervous as if wanting to impress us, I suppose. She didn't go into detail about her life before she cleaned up but told us almost every detail of her life after she met Aiden and joined the Order of Greatness. She described Carey House in detail and wanted us to be just as excited about living there.

When Rachel wasn't talking, Kory would try to fill in the silent gap. She told Rachel about our accomplishments in school and our dance classes when we were younger. She told her about how I'd won MVP in softball every year for three years as a pitcher and about how we always competed with one another on stage during a ballet performance. She talked on and on about her day-to-day life with her friends.

I sat alone in the back seat with my book, feeling a little pang of jealousy. Kory was talking more to Rachel during this trip than she had spoken to me since the reading of the will – the only exception was our time spent packing. Granted, we'd been busy with the move. But for the first time in my life I felt like an outsider, like a third wheel, where my sister was concerned. Maybe one day Kory would be okay living with Rachel on her own. I spent most of the trip reading, writing in my journal, and listening to music on my iPhone. Rachel tried to make small talk with me, but soon gave up when I only offered her one-word answers.

It wasn't until we were about a mile away from our destination when the same feeling I had that day at the house with Pastor Simms emerged. I'd been lying across the backseat drifting in and out of sleep when the quaking started. I sat up. Kory was gazing out the window. Rachel was quiet now, so I decided not to bother either one of them, especially if it was another hallucination. I grabbed a bottle of water and leaned against the back of the seat. The quaking continued, and I blinked as my vision blurred.

I placed my forehead on the cool window glass. A figure stood on the side of the road. Even though the car was going at a speed of fifty-five miles per hour or so, it was the same figure over and over again like a movie projector image - an old white-haired man dressed in dark pants and a white button-down shirt, open at the collar and blood soaked down the front. His right arm leaned heavily on a cane as his left arm pointed at me. Since it was the same figure repeatedly, and with the car going as fast as it was, it appeared as if his arm moved - pointing in the direction we were traveling.

Then, everything went black.

CHAPTER EIGHT

I woke up to Kory shaking me. Apparently, she and Rachel thought I'd fallen asleep again. They had no idea of the horrifying image I'd seen, and I decided not to say anything to them.

More than likely, Rachel wouldn't believe me. She didn't even know me.

As for Kory, well, I didn't want to ruin her perfect day. For the first time in quite a while I had seen my sister smile. But deep inside I wondered, what does it all mean? Is it even real?

A demon.

The thought entered my mind so quickly and with such force, I looked around the backseat for a stranger. A man's voice had said the words so close to my ear, I imagined I'd felt hot breath on my skin. I looked at Kory as if seeing her for the first time.

She smiled. "We're here."

I got out of the car with legs shaking, but almost completely forgot about the vision of the old man as I stared up at Carey House. This was not just a house. It was everything Rachel had said, except it was almost a monstrosity. It was so large it could easily house twenty people. It seemed to grow larger by the second. I'd only seen pictures of places like this in Europe. Yet here it stood; our new home – half house, half castle. It reminded me of the medieval church from my dream, except much larger.

Coming out a wide oak door to meet us was a very well-dressed Aiden and I wondered if he ever took a day off and lounged around in jeans or shorts. Maybe flip flops? I stifled a laugh as Kory elbowed me, giving me an all too familiar of late warning to be nice.

Aiden immediately went to Rachel and pulled her close, giving her a hug. He whispered something in her ear as she smiled up at him. I began to realize how tired Rachel must be. She'd been driving for sixteen hours total. I'd never thought to offer to drive. Then again, she's the one that wanted us here in the first place. Why shouldn't she be the one to drive?

Aiden came over and grabbed both of us girls into a hug. I didn't know how to react, but Kory hugged him back tightly. I stared at the clone who had once been my sister.

"This is great that the two of you get to join us here at Carey House. Your rooms are ready, and I'll show you around. Rachel, why don't you head on up and get some rest. You look tired, baby."

Rachel smiled and did his bidding. After giving him a quick kiss on the cheek, she grabbed her handbag and disappeared into the monster size house.

"You can leave your bags here and Martha will come out to get them and take them to your rooms."

"Who is Martha?" I asked.

Kory leaned over and whispered, "Mom told us about her in the car, Ava." I shrugged. Probably during my black out.

"Martha Buckley is from the congregation, she is a member of the Order. I met her in Ireland a few years ago and she agreed to relocate here. She is also our housekeeper and keeps everything looking nice. She's fantastic. Plus, this way, your mom doesn't have to worry about trying to keep up with this huge place. We also have members who come in to do the landscaping." He surveyed the estate, narrowing his eyes at the bright sun. "We don't have to pay them. They do it all for the love of the Order."

Before I had a chance to ask him anything else about the Order and its members, he grabbed Kory and me around the shoulders, one on each side of him and led us over the grounds. His movement caught me off guard and I glanced at Kory. She didn't seem to mind his intrusiveness. She actually smiled at him as we walked.

To walk around this house - if that's what I should call it - was even more impressive. Bushes and flowers bloomed all the way around the stone block masonry of the building. Some flowers I recognized, but so many others belonged in another country; exotic looking flowers. The building was three stories high, at least, with long narrow windows. Lyle Carey based the architecture and the blueprints on a centuries-old church in England, according to Aiden.

As we moved around back, we saw a separate greenhouse past the gazebo. Kory practically jumped up and down, breaking our tight little row. "Is that a real greenhouse? Are you using it? Do you have plants in there?"

Aiden smiled amusingly at my little sister. "Yes, we grow many different plants and flowers here that you wouldn't otherwise see in West Virginia. We grow our own vegetables and herbs as well. You'll see a vegetable garden behind the greenhouse. Go ahead and have a look around. You can do whatever you want with the plants. I know Iris raised you to appreciate gardens. You're both probably better experts on plants than my people."

Kory gripped my wrist but then took off running leaving me behind with Aiden. She ran to the greenhouse and disappeared inside, but I could still see her faint movement behind the glass. Aiden and I still walked slowly towards the greenhouse, although I had put more distance between us, and I took a deep breath as I looked around. This was to be our home for the next two years if I could make it that long.

I was a little shocked when Aiden reached over and touched my arm making us pause in our walk. He looked down at me and for a moment I could see what Rachel saw in him. He was by far a good-looking man, charismatic and charming. His dark eyes bore intently into mine as if he was trying to read me. "Ava, your mom and I want to make a home here for you and Kory. It looks like your sister wants this as well. I hope you do too. You know, this is for the best. You shouldn't have the responsibility of raising a fifteen-year-old girl when you, yourself, should be finishing up school, thinking about college and the rest of your life. I really want you to open your mind up to what the Order can offer you and what this family can offer you. We have ways of opening many doors for you, but only if you're here in Webster Mills." He ran his hand up and down my arm.

I stared at him wondering if this was some type of threat or possibly a bribe. Was he saying if I didn't go along with the Order, I wouldn't get into college or have a future here in West Virginia? If I played the good girl, would I get everything I wanted? I looked down at his hand still on my arm and peered back up at him. He wore a charming smile on his clean-shaven face but seeming to sense that I may not fall for all his charms, he dropped his hand slowly from my arm.

Kory emerged from the greenhouse. "Ava, you've got to come see this. It is so amazing, Iris would have loved it!" Not looking back, I walked quickly to the greenhouse to join my sister.

Once inside, I saw just how dazzling a real greenhouse could be. There was such a variety of flowers and plants in a wide range of colors. Kory ran around one side of the greenhouse to the other mesmerized by all the flowers. The deluge of scents was a bit overwhelming for me and I started sneezing. As I took a step backwards, I fanned myself with my hand to keep the nausea at bay from the overpowering mixture of scents and the humidity in the greenhouse.

"Kory, I seriously need to go back outside. It smells good in here, but I am dying!" I turned towards the door and felt the burst of fresh air as I started back onto the path that led around the grounds. Aiden waited further up the path with an older man in deep conversation. I slowed down to wait for Kory. She came up the path with a small bouquet of flowers she handpicked.

"Aiden might get mad at you for picking those," I said under my breath, so he and the man wouldn't hear.

Kory rolled her eyes as we approached the two men. "No, he won't, Ava. He said we could take what we wanted."

Something was off about the older gentleman's appearance, his countenance, as we approached. His back was to me and he faced Aiden shifting back and forth from left to right as if missing his cane and forced to stand there without support. He wore black dress pants and an untucked white long-sleeved shirt which seemed odd considering how warm it was for a summer evening. The back of his head was oddly shaped with tufts of white hair poking out randomly, like the hair was simply an afterthought. I couldn't take my eyes off his head. As we got closer the man suddenly turned. He was only a few inches taller than me, but his lifeless eyes bore into mine all the same, dark sunken pits. No eyes. Only holes. The front of his shirt covered in blood. His contorting mouth opened, but I only heard my own screams.

I jumped back and grabbed Kory, but he was gone. She stood in his place now, anger crossing her face. Her eyes looked like burning amber when she was angry, unlike my own that resembled coal when pushed too far.

"What is wrong with you?" she demanded.

"The man, where did he go?" I moved around Kory to stand in front of Aiden. This had to be a trick from these Order people. If not, then not only had I seen it, it had seen me - twice. Three times, if I counted the experience back home.

"What man?" Aiden looked at me as if I was playing a game and snarled his mouth into a grin, but his eyes were lit up. "Ava, that kind of dramatic behavior is not tolerated here. Maybe we should sit down and have a family meeting to discuss your role here." His Irish accent thickened and the way he said the word family made me want to heave onto his fine shoes.

I looked over my shoulder at Kory. She was shaking her head while picking up the flowers I must have either knocked out of her hand or she dropped when I saw…whatever I saw. I leaned down and picked up a flower and handed it to her.

"You didn't see anyone, did you?" I asked her quietly.

She leaned in closer to my face, so Aiden couldn't hear. "I may or may not have heard a moaning the same time you screamed, but I didn't see anything." Her eyes searched my face, and then she stood and plastered on a smile for Aiden. The rest of the walk back consisted of Aiden telling more of the history of Carey House and the Order. I only caught bits and pieces of it. What Kory revealed was staggering. Had she heard the things I saw, but unable to see them? If that was true, we would have to work together to find out who this apparition of an elderly man with a blood-soaked shirt was haunting the grounds and why.

CHAPTER NINE

The house was every bit what Rachel alleged. Large and impressive, it looked more like a cathedral than a home. The downstairs consisted of an aptly named Great Hall with sparse furnishings, a dining room with a long table that sat twelve people, and an expansive kitchen that once upon a time was used to make large meals to feed dozens of people, according to our tour guide Aiden. A narrow hallway off from the Great Hall led to two doors. The one on the left was Aiden's office and library and the door on the right was the meeting room for the Order. He said we were not to go into either room unless told. The Meeting room was open during meetings but locked otherwise. His office stayed locked and only he and senior members, known as Elders, carried the key. Kory and I exchanged glances.

A grand marble staircase led to the second floor. Reminding me of a hotel, it held four large bedrooms with attached baths as well as a den.

"These rooms are huge, Aiden. Maybe a couple of my friends could visit and stay in one of these?" Kory's eyes lit up as she pointed to a guest bedroom on the right, complete with antique furnishings in a dark wood.

Aiden nodded his head. "We'll see. These bedrooms are for people visiting the Order or those needing a place to stay during a crisis. We try to keep them ready at all times."

As we climbed a much smaller marble staircase to the third floor right past the den, I wondered what constituted a crisis to this group. Homelessness? Natural disasters? A made-by-the-Order calamity?

Private bedrooms for the family were on the third floor. Kory's room was right of the stairs next to a door Aiden said led to the attic. Her suitcases and boxes were already on the floor, but the sheer magnitude of the room surprised me. It was larger than the previous guest rooms and outfitted with hand-carved antique furniture. The dark wood blended well with the thick door frames that seemed to decorate every room in the house. I'd assumed our bedrooms would be Harry-Potter-closet small and sparse considering we were teenagers coming to live here with such little notice.

Seeming to sense my awe, Aiden motioned us back out to the hall past a bathroom to my room. The color scheme was different than Kory's room. Hers was burgundy and gold with dark wood. My room had the same dark hardwood floor, however, with pastel greens and blues and white furniture. I walked out onto a balcony that looked over the side of the house towards the greenhouse, the gazebo, and a little pond. For an exquisite moment, I felt like a little girl again, a pretend princess. I could see landscaping and forest for miles. There was no hiding my excitement and pleasure for this room. I stepped back inside to find Rachel lounging across the four-poster queen-sized bed in shorts and a tank top and freshly washed hair. Kory flopped down next to her.

"I thought I heard the three of you come up," Rachel smiled and looked about the room. "Ava, I thought this room was perfect for you; very relaxing and breezy." She rolled off the bed and went to the balcony door for a moment breathing the fresh air in deeply.

"Oh, Ava, you have got to feel these beds! They are amazing." Kory made snow angel movements on the comforter.

Rachel laughed at Kory, a once familiar sound.

"Kory, do you like your room?" She asked.

Kory bolted up, her hair a tangled mess. "Yeah! It is so beautiful. I can't wait to have people over after I make new friends."

Rachel glanced over at Aiden, who was still leaning against the bedroom door frame, but neither spoke. His eyes flickered to me knowing I'd caught the exchange. Before I had a chance to say anything, Rachel was on the move. Apparently, her cat nap had reenergized her.

Down the hall a bit further were two more rooms across from one another. Rachel took us into the room on the left. It was by far the best and most breathtaking bedroom in the house. A massive round skylight was in the center of the room above a large four poster bed that had to be really old, maybe older than the house. Lion faces adorned the top of each post. Apart from the wooden furniture, everything was white in this room with yellow accents. Rachel announced proudly this was hers and Aiden's room. Kory and I were speechless.

"That is the same look your mother gave me when she saw it for the first time." Aiden leaned on the doorframe watching us. Rachel walked over to him and kissed him with such a passion, I blushed and turned away.

Kory and I in silent agreement gravitated toward one of the two balconies. This view was of the back of the house and I could see both cleared land marked with benches and shrubbery and a little farther out into the woods. The hillside to the left loomed over us as if trying to compete with the size of the house.

"One more room and I'll let you girls go unpack until dinner's done." We followed Rachel across the hall into a room only about half the size of our rooms. It had a dark wood floor and white walls, windows, but no balcony or bathroom. A ceiling fan was the only ornate thing in this room. Otherwise it was empty. Aiden went to one of the windows that overlooked the grounds as Rachel walked into the middle of the room and spun around like a ballerina who'd escaped her jewelry box but didn't know where to go.

"Aiden and I have decided to have a baby. This will be his room."

"Wow," Kory said as we both stood in shock. "Are you pregnant?"

"No, but we're doing everything we can to get that way!" Rachel said. When Aiden didn't answer or turn to look at us, Rachel switched gears on the awkward situation. "Well, this sums up your tour. Why don't you go ahead and get some unpacking done?"

We left the now-quiet couple in the unofficial nursery.

CHAPTER TEN

A fter dinner, Rachel and Aiden surprised me with a cake for my birthday. It was a strange celebration. We sat in the dining room eating while members of the Order came in and out of the house. Apparently, people mill around and work at Carey House all day. It made me nervous, so I ate very little.

I regretted it a few hours later. After spending more time unpacking and catching Freya up on the move through FaceTime, my stomach was rumbling - loudly. There was no way I could go to sleep with a growling belly, so I made my way down to the kitchen.

It was after nine o'clock and starting to get dark outside. The kitchen was quiet with no members in sight and I was thankful. The last thing I wanted to do was face a member bent on cleaning for their Order. The kitchen was immaculate. Although the house was old, the kitchen sported new stainless-steel appliances and marble countertops. Sandwich making materials filled the massive refrigerator, so I pulled them out one by one and spread them across the butcher block counter. I stuck my face back into the fridge when someone entered the kitchen. I backed out in time to see Jake Henderson turn the faucet on.

"Hey, Jake," I said, carrying a container full of sliced watermelon to the counter.

"Hope you don't mind. Aiden sent me in here, I haven't eaten all day." He dried his hands on a paper towel.

"Here, let me fix you something." Jake tried to refuse me, but I totally ignored him. "What do you like on your sandwich? They have everything. Rachel must feed a small army." Jake named off the items for his sandwich and then grabbed an apple from the counter and bit into it. I'd planned on taking my plate upstairs to eat, but instead I pulled out a stool from under the counter to sit and eat with him.

While I finished putting the last touches on his sandwich, he poured us each a glass of sweet tea with his apple stuck in his mouth. In one quick motion, he dropped the apple from his mouth into his hand, and then wiped the juice from his chin with the back of his hand.

"Can I ask you somethin'?" Jake asked as he pulled out the stool next to me, his cute brows knitted together in a question.

"Sure."

"Why do you call your mother by her first name?"

I set my sandwich down and took a drink of my tea. He didn't need to know the details of our family's past. "Kory and I lived with our aunt for the last eight years... I just don't call her Mom." I gave him a weak smile. "So why did you join the Order?"

Jake finished chewing his bite of sandwich. "My parents died in a car crash two years ago and I've been livin' with my uncle since. He's a good guy, but kind of goin' nowhere. He married and divorced young, had two kids who live with their mom. Now he has a fulltime job, a truck payment, a mobile home payment, and me." He shrugged. "I wanted somethin' more and Aiden's made that possible."

"How?"

"When I needed help in school my senior year, he arranged for tutors. He made one phone call and got me my first part time job. He went with me to the college when I applied to make sure I didn't have any problems with admissions or financial aid." He drank down his tea. "I guess I'm tryin' to understand why, if you have parents like Aiden and Rachel, you wouldn't acknowledge that?"

I pushed a piece of watermelon around on my plate with my fork. I didn't want to answer him too loudly in case someone overheard. "Being a parent is more than just giving material things and opening doors to opportunities. It's a sense of family and loyalty, being there when you don't have to be, but because you want to see your child grow up and succeed. We had that with our great-aunt Iris. When it comes to Rachel, I'm still working that part out."

Jake studied me for a moment, and then nodded his head. "Thanks for the great dinner. I need to head home." He took his plate and glass over to the sink. "Hey, I was thinking, if you're not doin' anything tomorrow, do you want to get out of the house and ride into the city? They have a Starbucks and a shopping mall. I could throw in for some pizza." His eyes sparkled when he talked.

"Sure, I'd like that. Can Kory come, too? She's about to go stir crazy."

"Of course." He started towards the kitchen door, and then turned, "By the way, happy birthday."

I smiled back. A year ago, today, I'd spent the entire day with Iris, Kory, and Freya at the mall. We'd shopped, got our nails done, and ate at an expensive Italian restaurant. Iris had surprised me with an ice cream cake for my seventeenth birthday. Then, we'd all stayed up and watched scary movies huddled in the living room floor.

I slowly crept upstairs alone to my new room.

Happy eighteenth birthday to me.

CHAPTER ELEVEN

The next morning, I pulled myself out of a sound sleep to sit up, breathless. I placed my shaking hand over my rapidly beating heart. I couldn't remember the dream, only the whispers of my name. I glanced at the stack of pillows, still trying to catch my breath and get my bearings.

That's right. Carey House. Our new home.

I threw myself back into the pillows and shut my eyes. Despite my aversion to this new life, the bed was the most comfortable I'd known.

I'm not sure how long I laid like that when I felt someone staring at me. I opened one eye, expecting to see Kory. The room was empty, and the door still shut. I turned over to face the door.

"*Ava.*"

I lunged for the floor, banging my knees against the hardwood. Ignoring the pain, I jumped to my feet, my hands up to defend myself.

There was no one there.

I touched my ear. Not only had I heard my name, I'd felt breath over my ear, as if someone was lying in the bed next to me.

I moved quickly out of the room and into the hallway. I stopped short in front of Kory's room at the top of the stairs. I could hear her voice, but it wasn't coming from her room. It sounded like she was on the second floor talking to someone. I slid quietly down each step trying to listen intently over my wildly beating heart. When I got to the landing I poked my head around. Kory stood at the doorway facing the second-floor den.

"Ava and I do appreciate staying here, but I'm really here to be close to Mom and to have a home. That's all. I'm so not interested in anything else, the Order, or otherwise." Someone said something to her I couldn't make out. Kory shifted backwards as if moving away from something.

"I need to finish getting dressed for breakfast," she said. I bolted quietly back up the stairs to my room. With my door opened slightly, I heard Kory shut her door and lock it.

I crept out into the hallway heading for Kory's room, but voices on the stairs stopped me cold. It was Aiden and Rachel. I rushed back to my room and threw my clothes on. Talking to Kory would have to wait.

Kory was already downstairs in the kitchen, pouring herself a cup of freshly brewed coffee by the time I looked presentable enough to face the members of the Order who seemed to be all over the first floor.

Strangely enough, none of the members were in the kitchen this morning, only Aiden and Rachel. Rachel looked beautiful in her blue plush robe, frilling around the kitchen frying eggs and bacon, stirring gravy, and baking biscuits. Aiden was sitting at the butcher block table reading something on his iPad. I nudged Kory as I grabbed a large red mug. The aroma from the coffee and the food made my stomach growl loudly and Kory made a face at me.

"Good morning, girls!" Rachel twirled about obviously proud of her breakfast making skills. "I'm making breakfast for the two of you since today is the first day of our little family."

Kory mumbled thanks and plopped down on the stool near Aiden. She was looking into her coffee mug and didn't see him frown.

"Kory," his voice low and controlled as she looked up from her mug. "Your mother got up early to prepare food for you, so you need to be a little more appreciative." Kory's eyes narrowed into her cup.

What was going on?

Aiden continued staring at Kory. After a long moment, she smiled and looked towards Rachel. "I'm sorry. I didn't mean to be rude. Thank you for breakfast."

"You're welcome, honey," Rachel answered her quietly.

I stood with my back against the counter, sipping my coffee. Aiden had gone back to reading and scrolling. He still hadn't said anything to me this morning. The kitchen was awkwardly silent with the exception of the sound of Rachel's whisk.

She was stirring the gravy and staring hard at the bubbly mixture. I kind of felt sorry for her. She was trying to assume her motherly role, a role she'd gladly given to Iris years ago.

"Well, it smells good," I said quietly. Rachel turned and smiled at me. She looked almost giddy and I prayed she wouldn't hug me for the compliment. I grabbed two plates and automatically filled one for my sister and then myself. As I sat down at the table across from Kory, we locked eyes.

"After we eat, come up to my room. I want to talk to you," I told her, and she nodded. At this, Aiden set his iPad down.

"Good morning, Ava," he said, apparently just noticing my presence. I smiled out of politeness.

Rachel served him a plate of food and as she was moving away he caught her wrist, smiled up at her and kissed it. She giggled like a schoolgirl before sitting down to her own plate across from him.

"Since I have both of you down here, I want to talk to you about school." Aiden took a long drink from his coffee mug. "Two of our members, Julia and Barb are retired teachers. They do some subbing in the public schools and tutor when needed. I've asked both of them to home school. They are very good, and of course, I will take care of the costs associated with it."

Kory and I had always attended public school. "Why do we need to be home schooled? Is there something wrong with the school system here?" I asked.

Rachel placed her hand on mine. "No, no, nothing like that, Ava. Aiden and I think it best for you two to have more one on one attention. We want to give you the best and we believe this will help your scores for exams…for college."

The word *Liar* crossed my mind.

"I'm not going to be home schooled by some weird fanatics of I don't know what," Kory shook her head. Her gaze was steady and aimed at Aiden.

Aiden leaned back on his stool. It appeared that he was sizing up my sister, although he didn't seem angry that Kory had blatantly slammed the Order.

Finally, after a long awkward silence, Aiden jumped up. "I do have something for you," he said and went to the pantry.

He pulled out a small purple bag. When he sat back down at the table he removed two white boxes out of it. He handed Kory and me each one. The box revealed a charm bracelet. I had to admit the bracelet was beautiful. It had silver, gold, and two-tone beads as well as colored beads of different shades of red. The charms were unique, too. One was an owl with red eyes and another one in the shape of a quill. Before I could ask about the charms, Rachel chimed in running her perfectly polished nail across the beads I held in the palm of my hand.

"We tried to pick out charms that would mean something to each of you. I based them on the pictures from Iris and from our talk in the car. Aiden took care of the rest." She must have meant Kory then, because as memory served, I'd done little talking to her that day.

Kory reached across the table. "Let me see yours." We exchanged the bracelets. Hers had different shades of blue and one of the charms was a ballerina. Rachel had done well. This one fit Kory to a tee. As I handed hers back Kory held my gaze a little longer.

Something was wrong.

I swallowed hard. "Thank you. It's beautiful." Was all I could get out as I quickly glanced at Aiden. I expected Kory to say thank you, but instead she placed the bracelet back in the box and slowly slid it across the table to Rachel.

"Mom, this is really nice and well thought out. But it kind of feels like a bribe. I don't want to be homeschooled here by members of your Order and I'm sure Ava feels the same way." Kory nodded her head in my direction. I nodded in agreement and put my bracelet back in its box, too.

Was this some type of bribe? Everything was happening too fast, especially these last two weeks. Before today, Kory was on my case about not giving Rachel and this place a shot. Now here I sat dazzled by a piece of jewelry while my sister was the Questioning One.

Rachel sat back in her chair stunned and appeared a little hurt by Kory Ann's accusation. Before she could say anything, Aiden was up and around the table in a matter of seconds. "A bribe?!" His voice teetered on staying within normal limits. He glared hard at Kory as he spoke, his Irish accent thickening.

"A bribe for wha', Kory? We are trying to make a safe home for you here with the best of everything, including an education. All we ask is that you are appreciative of the lil' things."His voice hissed in an effort to maintain control. "Plus, Ava's bracelet is for 'er birthday." He placed both hands on Rachel's shoulders as she stared down at her plate of uneaten biscuits and gravy.

I took a deep breath. "Aiden, we don't want to be homeschooled or join the Order. We thought we were clear on this before we left home." His focus turned to me and at once I saw rage and hatred in his devilish eyes.

He might be mad at Kory, but I enraged him. This probably would scare most girls my age. Heck, Rachel wouldn't even look up from the table. My insides shook as we glared at each other.

Aiden shut his eyes and took a deep breath. Kory and I exchanged glances. She was right. We'd told Aiden and Rachel we would come live with them because Kory had no choice, but we were not going to join the Order of Greatness. This was just another ploy to introduce it to us.

He opened his eyes. "Let's just finish breakfast and we can talk more about this at dinner." He walked slowly all around the table and as he passed he placed his hand on my shoulder. At once, I felt a static charge and he jerked his hand away. I looked up at his surprised expression.

We finished breakfast in silence.

CHAPTER TWELVE

After breakfast, Kory and I went straight to my room to talk about the morning's happenings behind closed doors. It was a relief to get away from Aiden and Rachel. The whole controlling parent thing was starting to feel downright weird. Iris was one thing, family. Rachel had a lot to prove. As for Aiden…

"By the way, who were you talking to this morning?" I opened a box and started unwrapping glassware from the house in North Carolina. Kory shrugged her shoulders as she pulled a newspaper wrapped vase out of the box.

"I thought I heard voices on the second floor, so I walked down there, but Aiden was the only one in the den. I don't know. Sometimes he just creeps me out." She sat down on the side of my bed holding the red Fenton vase that was at least seventy years old. She stared at it through glazed eyes.

"What do you mean sometimes he creeps you out?" Maternal instinct for my sister kicked in.

"Aiden was standing in the den facing the wall and I swear he'd been talking to someone, but no one was there. He turned around and saw me before I had a chance to get back upstairs. I don't know, sometimes it's the way he looks at me. I can't tell if he is being nice or..." Her voice trailed off.

"Kory Ann, look at me." I sat down next to her on the bed. "Tell me the truth, did he try something? If he did, you have got to tell me."

"No. He just looked at me weird. I don't know. I don't want to talk about it anymore." She got off the bed and placed the vase on the tall dresser near the corner of the room. "There, that's better, don't you think?" She moved the old vase around until it was center.

Remembering the voice in my ear this morning, I decided now was the best time to get to the bottom of Kory's experiences since Iris's death.

"What have you heard this past week? I mean, like when I passed out at home when Pastor Simms was there and in the car on the way here? Did you hear anything? You said you heard something outside the greenhouse yesterday." Kory's eyes grew dark as she looked at me. She plopped down at the foot of the bed and sighed dramatically. Typical Kory.

"I didn't want to tell you because all of this seems is like a dream come true. Mom showing up to bring us home, and not just any home, but here." She waved her hand in the air and then a sad look crossed her face. "I've been hearing strange voices and sounds. Some are friendly, and others are terrifying. I thought I heard someone talking to Aiden in the den. At first, I thought I was imagining it, but now I'm not so sure. Maybe too much stress, like Pastor Simms said."

Although Kory appeared a little shaken, I couldn't have been happier. This meant I wasn't crazy, not yet, and what I saw was real because my sister heard the same things that I saw. My head hurt just thinking about it.

"I've been seeing things since the funeral. At first, I thought it was just my way of coping with losing Iris, but this morning I heard my name whispered in my ear and felt a breath on my skin. You said you heard Aiden talking to someone that wasn't there this morning. I wonder if I had been there if I would've seen who he was talking to. Outside the greenhouse, when you heard that scream, he'd been talking to a man covered in blood".

Kory's eyes grew wide.

I got off the bed and went out to the balcony. I needed some fresh air. I needed to think. What could it all mean? I gripped the cast iron railing and felt the coolness of the metal as my thoughts swirled. I turned to face the French doors. Kory hadn't moved. After a moment, she smiled.

"Ava? I have an idea. If we stick together maybe we can find out what is really happening here. For now, I can hear them, and you can see them, but it's like listening to a sound through pillows. It's muffled. And this morning you heard and felt something. What if we can make it clearer, stronger? What if, whatever this is, Iris knew about it and that's why she called Mom?" Excitement replaced the fear and sadness from earlier.

The visions weren't crystal clear either. It was like looking at an old mirror left out in the rain. "As the older sib I feel the need to point out to you this might be dangerous. All of this started when Iris died. Maybe you're right. Maybe she knew something." I walked back into the room as an idea crossed my mind and I felt a cold chill. "What if we aren't the only ones seeing and hearing things? Do you think Rachel does?" I thought about when Aiden touched my shoulder and the look of shock on his face.

Kory bit her lower lip. "It's crazy, but I feel like we should already know about this. Do you remember Iris saying anything before?"

I crossed the floor of the bedroom as I tried to remember things Iris had said, but I couldn't sort a lifetime of conversations. Had she said something subtly? There was no way of knowing.

"We'll have to go back to the house. We need to go and look through her things. We didn't go into detail in her room when we packed. All the important documents were in her desk. Maybe she left other papers or a journal."

Kory shook her head. "Do you really think Aiden and Mom are going to let us travel back to look for some of Iris' things? They'll want to know why we need to go now."

A sudden and brilliant plan flashed through my mind like a lightning bolt. "They will let us go because someone is going to break into the house."

Kory smiled and pulled her cell phone from her back pocket.

CHAPTER THIRTEEN

I sent Jake a text letting him know Kory and I couldn't make it to the mall today. I left out the part about our mission to get back home. A quick Facetime call to Kory's teenage suitor Dillon and the plan was set into motion.

By evening, Dillon scoped out the house to make sure no one was around. As far as we knew the caretaker was to only show up on Saturdays to keep the lawn care up and check on the house. Dillon called us back before dinner to tell us "someone" had thrown a rock through the dining room window. No one saw him. When he asked why we needed him to damage our personal property, Kory, being his crush since ninth grade, told him it was a secret and when she saw him soon she would fill in the blanks.

"Let me know if there is anything I can do to get you back home," Dillon said as he took off his ballcap to wipe the sweat off his face. His massive mane of dark hair blotted out his face on Kory's iPhone.

"Oh, don't worry. You'll be the first to know," Kory said and winked.

My sister, always the flirt.

We stayed in our rooms through lunch. Members of the Order were downstairs and neither one of us wanted to deal with them. Hours later after everyone left, starving, we joined Aiden and Rachel for dinner in the dining room. We all sat at one end of the table with Aiden at the head, this morning's squabble apparently forgotten. The chat was mostly about the Order or how much we unpacked in our rooms.

Halfway through dinner the phone in the kitchen rang and Aiden got up to answer it. Kory and I looked at each other knowing it was the authorities on the phone. When Aiden came back into the dining room, he wore a frown on his face.

"Someone broke into Iris' house. The police said it didn't look like anything was taken, but I am going to have a security system installed. Maybe have the caretaker stop by there twice a week." He sat back down at the table.

Before I had a chance to say anything about going to the house, Rachel jumped in. "I think we should go down there and check, Aiden. No one would have broken into Iris' place without a reason."

Aiden shook his head and placed a hand on Rachel's. "They said nothing was taken. There's no need."

I don't really remember our mother before we were taken from her, only in glimpses, but I felt something familiar just then. She was studying Aiden intently and quietly. The air in the room seemed to shift. He continued to stare at her with his hand on hers.

Suddenly, Rachel broke the silence and spoke quietly and slowly. "Aiden, I think we should go to the house and see if anything was taken.

Things the authorities never knew were there." Aiden jerked his hand away from her and stood up, almost knocking his chair over.

"I'll book us a flight for in the mornin'." He left the room and Kory and I looked at each other startled. Rachel pushed her plate away and turned in her chair to face Kory and me. Oddly, she stuck her index finger in her glass of water. Kory, who was seated next to her, leaned away as if getting ready to receive a blow.

That's when I felt it.

A hot blast of air hit me, and my hair moved away from my face. It was coming from Rachel whose face was stone as she scowled at us.

"I want to know what you two did to Iris' house and why and I want to know now." I could feel myself getting sick to my stomach from the constant flow of heat emanating from Rachel. I bent forward, dry heaved, my head pounding. I tried to move off my chair, to stand up, to get out of the room, but it was as if a large hot hand held me in place. I couldn't see Kory through my tears.

Rachel asked again. "I want you to tell me what you did to the house. Why would someone break in?" My heavy head swooned, and I felt it lower to the table. If an answer was what she wanted I couldn't give her one even if I tried. My throat parched from the heat, my body only moments from combusting.

Then I heard Kory's voice from a distance. "We're seeing and hearing things…not there. We thought we'd find something…at the house…to help us."

Suddenly the blast of heat was replaced with fresh cool air. Too late. I vomited my dinner onto the floor beside my chair. When I could finally look up, Rachel was watching me. She didn't look angry now, only sad. Kory downed her glass of water. I took her cue and did the same with my glass. I gulped it down quickly hoping it would settle my stomach and get the taste out of my mouth. It didn't. I'd never been so thirsty.

With my immediate physical concerns out of the way, I started to think clearly. Rachel had done something to us. Not with some wand or chant or crystal, but with a power coming from *within* her.

As if to sense my light bulb moment, Rachel rested her chin on the palms of her hands as if observing a movie about two monkeys. "I'm sorry, but I was afraid of this. Iris said she sensed that you both had power in you, but she didn't know how much or what abilities you had. Aiden is coming. We'll talk later in Kory's room. There's a great deal I need to tell you, I guess."

Before we could ask any questions, Aiden returned. He wasn't thrilled about the vomit on the floor.

CHAPTER FOURTEEN

That night in Kory's room, the three of us curled up on the bed. Although Kory and I had done this millions of times, we'd never had mother-daughter time with Rachel, so it was awkward. Now here we were waiting to learn what she knew, what powers she had, and where they came from.

Rachel stretched out across the bed with her long blonde hair swept to one side with a look ready to spill secrets. She'd told Aiden she felt closer to her girls and wanted to spend some time with us tonight, and he gave her some room. He said he had work to do in his office to prepare for the next Meeting anyway.

"Did Iris say anything to you about abilities or powers?" Rachel asked.

We both shook our heads. Kory answered, "No, when she was on hospice she told us about you, your past, but she never said anything about powers."

"She didn't," I added. "But, towards the end she was on a lot of pain medication. She couldn't stay awake for very long."

Rachel thought for a moment. "What abilities have you been able to do so far?"

"I've been seeing visions since the funeral and I've started hearing whispers. I actually felt something this morning brush by my hair like someone breathing on me." Rachel listened as I told her about my visions here and in North Carolina, but I noted she didn't seem surprised at all.

"Kory Ann?"

Kory pulled one of her pillows onto her lap. She looked like a little lost girl. "I've been hearing things, voices. I heard a scream out near the greenhouse the day we got here."

Rachel nodded. "Your abilities are still developing, and they will for some time. The younger you are the weaker your focus."

"We wanted to go to the house to see if Iris had left behind a clue, if she had known about any of this." I pulled at a loose string on the comforter.

Rachel was quiet for a moment. "When Iris came and took you girls, I knew it was for the best. I couldn't take care of you because I was strung out. I was doing drugs, hard core drugs, and your father taught me how to cook to make our own using a broken light bulb on the stove. I had power then, but I couldn't focus it because I had too much junk in my system. The power must be focused, and your mind and body must be in its best possible health. Even a sickness like pneumonia can throw your abilities off. And, of course, cancer... ."

After a moment, she took a deep breath. "The last straw for Iris was when she came to get you and she saw me. She cried. I cursed her because she was taking you, but I knew it was the right thing to do. It was four years before I could get enough strength to seek help. By then, I thought my powers were gone."

I interrupted her, "Why did you even get involved in drugs in the first place?"

Rachel did a small laugh and stared at the comforter as she answered. "Believe it or not, I thought the drugs would open my mind to have more power. I thought I could yield it somehow. But it's all a delusion really. It destroys your mind and your body." She looked genuinely sad when she said this and part of me felt for her. Kory must have felt the same way because she reached over and touched Rachel's hair. I think this surprised Rachel a little, but she smiled.

"When I met Aiden, I was a mess. He took pity on me, I think. He taught me about the Order and their belief that I could heal. I needed to be strong and get rid of all this emotional baggage. Once I was clean from the drugs and started eating healthy and taking care of myself, the powers started coming back. A little at first, then stronger. I should have realized the powers were there when I met Aiden, but I couldn't see it before. You've seen Aiden. A man like him is not going to stop on the street and offer to help a thirty-year-old homeless woman clearly on a drug who hasn't bathed in a week. It was the power that attracted him to me." She smiled wistfully at me. "I'm glad it did. But, Aiden doesn't know about our powers. He thinks everything that has happened has something to do with the Order and whatever secrets he possesses. And he is to continue thinking that."

Before I could ask her what secrets the Order hid, Kory jumped in. "Where do those powers come from, Mom? We need to know about them because sometimes what I hear is really scary and Ava has seen men in bloody clothes." She sank deeper into the bed as if she'd scared herself thinking about it.

This time Rachel sat up and crossed her legs. "This power was passed down through the women in our family. Some say it went back four hundred years, but I think it goes back further. Have you ever heard of a Siren? The Siren's Call? A mythological creature who lived in the water?"

"Sure," I knew mythology almost like the back of my hand thanks to English Lit class and Mr. Dawson's love affair with The Odyssey. However, Kory shook her head.

Rachel continued. "Sirens were female creatures who would lure sailors from their ships using their beauty and voices to trap the men. At least that is the story. Many people thought Sirens were prostitutes and sailors were their customers who would end up being broke by the time the women were done with them. And I'm sure there were cases like that. However, our family has a different story."

"The women in our family were given a special power to keep demons away from the villages. The demons preferred to inhabit men, so the 'Sirens' as they were called, were sent out to lure the men. They would then test them to see if they had the demon in them. If the man was possessed by the demon, the woman known as an Elemental, would kill him."

"Kill him? That's extreme. Couldn't the man be saved?" I shifted uneasily in the bed.

"In order for the man to be truly possessed, he had to have given himself over to his wants and desires before the demon could take over, leaving his soul wide open. So, no, once possessed the man was doomed." We sat quietly for a moment.

Rachel continued. "We can see the demons in both their present state and the past. We can hear the voices of the doomed men as well as those creatures. We attract men by giving out a sort of charge, kind of like the way certain foods can make you happy by increasing endorphins. At our strongest we can control the elements; earth, wind, fire, water. We are stronger near water however. That's why Iris kept her home near the ocean. Even just a few hours are enough to recharge us. That's the reason I asked Aiden to have a pond built on the grounds. I feed off the energy from the water and you do, too. Tell me, after the funeral, did you go down to the beach at all?"

Kory and I both nodded our heads. To get out of the house and away from packing we had gone one afternoon to Holden Beach. It wasn't crowded, and we sat with our chairs pulled up into the water, occasionally jumping in for a swim. It was so calming. It felt like home.

"We went for a few hours."

"That's all it takes when your power is developing. I can almost bet you Iris would take you to the beach on vacation for a week or two a year, didn't she? She actually rented a beach house, right?" When we nodded, she smiled. "Iris would have needed to recharge herself, especially if she had used a great deal of power earlier."

"So, Iris was a Siren?" I asked.

"Iris was an Elemental, just like you. Men throughout history called us Sirens because of the way our powers lured them." Rachel corrected.

"How do we control our powers, hone them?" Kory asked.

"I'll show you, but I do want us to go to Iris' house. We can double check and make sure Iris didn't leave anything that may tell people what we are. Plus, it will give us a chance to go to the ocean. I want to show you something. And remember this is one of the reasons boys will always want to talk to you and girls will despise you."

"Well, that explains seventh grade," I said and Kory snorted.

"Elemental energy and your health work hand in hand. So, get your sleep. Aiden says we fly out in the morning, so just pack for a few days and don't forget your swimsuits." And with that, Rachel kissed us both on our heads and bounded out of the room. She'd left the two white boxes on the bed with the bracelets inside.

My head swam with all this new information as I took my bracelet and slid it onto my wrist. I made it back to my room and crawled into the ginormous bed, but I couldn't sleep. Instead I grabbed my tablet from the nightstand and winced as the bright light temporarily blinded me in the dark. Maybe I should read up on the Siren myth and learn more about Elementals.

It sounded incredible, but it felt true and that was scary. We were Elementals sent to destroy demons.

But, why now? And, even scarier, how?

CHAPTER FIFTEEN

After a long while of researching multiple myths throughout time, I slumped back on the bed and closed my eyes.

I still didn't trust the Order, but any time I tried to talk to Rachel about them, she shut me down. "They're good people, Ava," she would say in her country accent. How could they be good people if their techniques were to brainwash people? The Order had so much pull on higher ups that in any other circumstance, it would be a cult, especially in a Bible belt area like West Virginia.

But, no one questioned them.

No one questioned Aiden.

The secrets surrounding the Order were well guarded under lock and key. Aiden kept both the Meeting room and his office locked at all times and only certain members went in outside of those times. And of course, there were always members floating around the first floor throughout the day.

I turned over in the bed, my mind racing. What if I could find out about the Order and their secrets? Not from members who would simply skew the truth, but the deep secrets that maybe they didn't know. I needed to get into the Meeting room.

Before I could change my mind, I slipped out of my room and across the hall. I'd noticed during our house tour that Aiden kept his wallet and keys on a tray on the dresser right inside his and Rachel's bedroom door. As I opened their bedroom door, the voice inside my head screamed. Of all the bad ideas I had ever concocted, this definitely topped the list. What if one of them woke up? I could picture Rachel glaring at me through sleepy eyes and causing me to accidently combust, or worse, Aiden waking up. I didn't want to think about what Aiden might do if he caught me stealing the key. I peered into their room. The moonlight from the enormous skylight shone on their bed like a beam. I could just make out Rachel's blonde hair near Aiden's shoulder.

I shut their door back. No, I would try to open the door with my power. If Rachel emanates a power, a force, then Kory and I probably do too. If it worked, it would be less dangerous than waking either one of them. Unless, I inadvertently set myself on fire.

Due to the size of the house it took me a few minutes to get to the smaller hallway off from the Great Hall, but it was quiet. None of the members stayed the night at Carey House, although the guest bedrooms were always ready.

I debated which room I should try first, the Meeting room or Aiden's office. I decided on the Meeting room first. It was a portion of the house much older than the rest and built specifically for the purpose of the Order. I laid my hand on the thick oak door expecting the wood to feel cool. It didn't. The door actually exuded unnatural warmth from it. I placed my face against the door and listened. I could have sworn the door breathed. I was beginning to let my imagination get the best of me.

I wrapped my fingers around the oblong door handle, feeling its ornate scrolling around the border underneath my grip, and squeezed the lever. Of course, the door did not open, did not budge.

I pushed harder. Still nothing. I closed my eyes as my insides began to shake. If I could control the visions, channel them, maybe I could focus long enough to open the door. The more I centered my focus, the more my core shook and burned - the energy building and threatening to escape if I wasn't careful. Instinctively, I placed both hands on the door, but kept my eyes squeezed tightly shut. I knew somehow if I opened them I would see an apparition standing to my left, inches from my face. I could already hear the raspy breath. Not wanting to know if it was there to warn me or stop me, I pushed harder on the door.

I heard a click as the door swung open and a blast of cool air hit my face. I opened one eye to confirm the Meeting room door stood open and listened for footsteps. Hurriedly, I stepped in and shut the door, praying that Aiden and Rachel wouldn't wake up and come downstairs.

Feeling around in the dark, I finally found a light switch. Why didn't I think to bring a flashlight? Then again, I didn't even know where Rachel kept them.

The large room lit up and I jumped at the brightness. No wonder the Order preferred to light candles when they met. A dust bunny couldn't hide in this stone room if it tried. I ran up onto the stage and behind the podium, scaring myself once when I caught a glimpse of a crazy girl in a pink pajama short-set on stage in the large mirror that hung on the wall. I waved at my reflection before I began to rifle through the podium. The podium was full of little cubby holes with a row of drawers at the bottom. I started rifling through the drawers first, filled with things used for the meetings; Aiden's notes, a few pieces of cloth with strange symbols on them, candles, a lighter. I got down on my knees and started looking in the little nooks. Most were empty, and others filled with everyday items like pens. All this work and I could find nothing in here to confirm my suspicions about the Order.

I sat back and scanned the room. I would need to get into Aiden's office next. I stood up to head to the door when something flashed to my right. Scaring me half to death, at first, I thought it was a camera flash.

All this sneaking around only to get caught by a picture?

On closer inspection, I realized the flash was coming from a crack in the stonework behind the stage. The crack was thin, but I managed to push my fingers into the cranny while standing on my toes. I could feel the sharp stone in the crevice and hoped my fingers were not disturbing a spider nest or some other gross creature. I pushed harder, feeling some of the rock crumble.

What was that? I wiggled my fingers. Paper? I pushed my hand a little deeper into the crevice, sliding my wrist into the hole while standing painfully en pointe. Thank God for all those ballet classes. Two of my fingers wrapped around the paper and I pulled. Nothing happened.

I realized one of the dangling charms on my bracelet was stuck in the crevice.

Really?

As I pulled harder, I struggled not to lose the paper still held by only two fingers. I dropped down allowing my heels to touch the floor, scraping my wrist across the stone crack. I could feel the paper in my grasp and pushed with my knee against the wall. Finally, part of the stone crevice crumbled and my hand wrenched free. The little scroll of paper fell to the floor and I snatched it up.

I silently made my way back to my room, listening for Aiden over the thudding in my chest, the scroll tucked neatly in my shorts in case I did run into him. I wanted to wait until I got to my room to read it behind closed doors. Whatever the paper contained had to be important for someone to go to all the trouble of hiding it in a stone wall.

Once in my room with the door locked, I slipped down beside the bed with my back against the wall, facing the door. What if Aiden burst through the door to find me reading the paper? My paranoia was running rampant.

I unrolled the small scroll only to see more of the symbols from the Meeting room. The symbols were strange anyway but looking at the paper I realized why they seemed odd. It was the arrangement on the paper; left to right, spaced evenly apart, rows and rows of them. It was a letter written in symbols. A code of some sort.

I grabbed my tablet off the bed and Googled 'strange symbols', but none of the images listed popped up. I tried more searches with words like 'alien', 'cult', and 'cultural'. None of the search results matched the symbols on the paper. I needed to find out what it all meant, but how?

After copying some of the symbols into my journal, I slipped the scroll into my jewelry box underneath a long watch case and dropped my bracelet on top before crumpling into bed for the night. It seemed like hours before I finally fell asleep.

CHAPTER SIXTEEN

Since we'd only be gone for a few days, Kory and I each packed a bag of clothes and a small bag of hair and makeup stuff. We waited by the front door in the Great Hall. I didn't say much to Kory this morning. I was too exhausted from my adventure into the Temple of Doom last night, plus I wasn't sure what to tell her. I didn't have a clue what the symbols meant.

When Aiden came downstairs with Rachel carrying their bags he smiled cheerfully at both of us.

"I can't believe I get to be seen with the likes of you three beauties." He set the bag down and kissed Rachel on the cheek. She was back to gawking at him as if he ruled the world. This led him to kiss her on the mouth and now I was done. I'd sat down on the bottom step of the large curving staircase, but with this show of PDA I decided to go back upstairs and grab a book to take with me on the flight.

"Where are you off to, Ava?" Aiden asked, his arms still wrapped around Rachel.

"I'm going to get a book."

"Don't forget to wear your bracelet," he added, before going back to snuggling with Rachel. She shook her right wrist at me and a charm bracelet jingled. Apparently, she had one from Aiden too. I glanced over at Kory, but she had her earphones in and iPhone turned up looking out the window close to the door.

I went to my room, found a book to read that would last me the round trip on the plane, and plucked the bracelet from my box. Although the bracelet was in my favorite color, it didn't match today's outfit - a pair of jeans and a hot pink tee with matching flip flops.

Whatever.

On second thought, I grabbed the small scroll from under the case and slipped it into my pocket. Maybe Iris had left something behind that would explain the symbols.

Somehow, I didn't think Aiden cared what I wore. He wanted all three of us wearing what he had given us. I sighed at this realization. Whether or not Rachel could see it, even with her powers, Aiden was controlling.

~ ~ ~

Roger Carter showed up and drove us in a BMW to the airport. This way he could take the car back to the house. Aiden told him when to meet us at the airport again in three days. The flight was shorter than I thought, and I wondered why we hadn't flown to West Virginia in the first place instead of driving all those hours. Maybe Rachel had wanted to spend time with us.

"Nervous about the flight?" Aiden asked as he and Rachel sat down to buckle into their seats directly across the aisle from me. Kory and I had fought over the window seat, but she'd won this round.

"Not really. We've flown before," I answered. "What happened to your hand?" The top of Aiden's right hand was wrapped in a fresh bandage that I knew wasn't there earlier.

"I accidently cut it before we left."

"It must be a bad cut from the size of the bandage."

He shrugged. "It's only across here," he pointed across his knuckles. "I need to pay closer attention to what's going on around me. It's a lesson to always stay vigilant." As odd an answer as that was, I quickly forgot about Aiden's hand when the small airplane's engine started. The plane flying out of Yeager Airport was much smaller than the ones I'd traveled in with Iris and Kory on our trips to Disney.

Aiden rented a car at the Charlotte airport and we drove to the house, our home. At once I felt better. Kory and I were the first ones out of the car; she already had her key out and in the door before I had my foot on the front porch.

For a house locked up for a few days, it still smelled of Iris; of comfort and coffee and hot cinnamon raisin bread. I wanted to cry. After walking through the house and viewing the boarded-up dining room window, I went out to the backyard. The caretaker was doing a good job. The flower and herb gardens looked great. Everything was neat, as if Iris was still here.

As I leaned down to look at a blooming red flower I saw it; a glint of glass in the soil. I moved it with my finger taking care not to cut myself. It was a shard from a mirror, maybe three inches long. And although I removed it from the rich soil, it wasn't dirty or muddy.

It looked as if someone placed it there. Why would the caretaker leave a piece of mirror behind in the soil? The only other person here had been Dillon, but he was in and out of the yard. He would have no interest in even glancing at the flowers.

Suddenly, my stomach churned, and I thought I might lose control of myself. I held the mirror tightly in my hand as my whole body began to tremble. The sky above appeared to grow dark as I fell to my knees in severe pain, and then dropped onto my back.

I raised my right hand in front of my face. Blood dripped from my clenched fist holding the mirror shard and ran down my wrist onto the charm bracelet. I took my left hand and forced my right one open. I had no control over the muscles in my right hand. When I could see the mirror shard, I pulled it out of my hand where it was lodged and gasped for air as another wave of pain shot through my body. As I held the shard with my quivering left hand, I gasped even louder.

In the bloody reflection I could see a dark creature. It was in the form of a man with horns. I dropped the glass and rolled over. My body shook while my mind started to darken. I closed my eyes and felt the dirt and grass on my lips.

And I could feel the creature's darkness coming nearer.

~ ~ ~

I woke to Aiden leaning over me with Rachel bandaging my right hand. I immediately tried to use my other arm to raise myself up, but Aiden pushed me back down on the couch with his hand on my chest near my throat. I grabbed at his wrist. I already felt like I was suffocating.

"Stop it, Ava. Hold still," he said.

I looked around. A bloody washcloth and a bottle of water sat on the coffee table next to Rachel. Kory leaned down from Aiden's shoulder. She could put on a good front, but her eyes showed it all. I'd scared her.

"Ava, what happened out there?" She whispered.

"I don't know. I found a piece of a mirror in the flower bed."

Rachel finished wrapping my hand and patted the top of it. "That must have been what you cut yourself on. There was so much blood I was afraid you'd accidently cut your wrist." She looked up at Aiden who was perched on the side of the couch with me. "Did you find glass out there?"

He shook his head, studying my face as if I might go into a convulsion any moment. "No, but I didn't really look around. I just grabbed her up and carried her into the house."

Rachel raised herself off the floor with a sigh. "I guess we should go look. I don't want anyone else to cut themselves. Two people in one day is more than enough."

When Aiden got up from the couch, I tried to sit up a bit, but Kory took his place. She touched my hand.

"Shouldn't we take Ava to the hospital? Wasn't she having a seizure or something? This isn't the first time."

I shook my head no. I didn't feel it was a real health concern. My body was having a reaction to…what? Demons? I tried not to think about the creature in the mirror.

"No, it will be alright. I think she is just tired. We've had a crazy couple of weeks and being back here probably overwhelmed her. Isn't that right, Ava?" Rachel asked and I nodded my head.

Aiden, who was standing in the doorway, did not look entirely convinced. "We probably shouldn't have come back yet. It's too soon for the girls. We'll leave t'morrow. I'll change the flights."

I waited until I heard the back door squeak shut before I sat up fully on the couch forcing Kory to move to the other end.

"You didn't find a shard of glass or sliver of mirror out there when you found me?" I asked her quickly, hoping Aiden and Rachel would be out there for a long while.

"I didn't find you. I was in my room when I heard a commotion. Aiden said he saw you fall flat on your face on the ground. He carried you inside. Your arm was covered in blood." She pointed at the washcloth and small bowl of reddish colored water on the table.

"I went to check on the backyard and found a small piece of a mirror in the flower bed. It wasn't dirty or anything, like someone just placed it there. When I picked it up I had one of those visions and I couldn't open my hand. That's how I got cut. When I finally did get to look at it I saw something in the mirror… and it wasn't me."

Kory pulled her legs up to her chest, her eyes wide. "What did you see?"

"It wasn't human. Or at least it wasn't *wearing* a human." I leaned over to Kory when I heard the screen door open.

I whispered, "I think I saw a demon."

CHAPTER SEVENTEEN

After Aiden and Rachel searched the backyard and flower garden to no avail, they gave up. The mirror shard was missing, and I couldn't remember what happened to it when I passed out. The only thing on my mind was the reflection. It was a dark and grotesque figure with a snarl across its lips. Was it a warning? Was I no longer seeing apparitions, but full-fledged demons now?

Rachel and I headed into Iris' room for anything regarding the Elementals. Kory searched the kitchen and pantry since Iris spent a great deal of time in there. Although he and Rachel would sleep in Iris' old room, unaware of the real reason for our visit, Aiden stayed in the living room talking on his cell to various members of the Order. Apparently, there was a great deal planned for the next meeting and this was a bad time for him to leave for North Carolina. He also planned to meet with a real estate agent about purchasing property in the Locklyn area for the Order, adding to their apparent and ever-growing stable of assets.

I rummaged through Iris' dresser looking for anything out of the ordinary. Nothing. Everything in her drawers I expected of an elderly woman who took good care of herself; clothes from boutiques and jewelry from the fine jewelry stores. Rachel pulled the nightstand drawer out and laid it on the bed, but nothing out of the ordinary; paperback books, reading glasses, a devotional. Nothing said our eighty-year-old great aunt lured men and vanquished demons. Rachel scanned the room from the bed with her bottom lip stuck out.

She turned quickly in my direction. "Where did Iris keep the vacation pictures?"

"You mean the ones from the beach?"

"Yes, any vacation pictures near water." Rachel leaped off the bed and began feeling the wall as if trying to see through it.

"She kept the photo albums in the linen closet in the dining room." I said. We quietly walked past the living room and overheard Aiden still on the phone. He sounded friendly, but firm regarding something about "how to deal" with another member.

Before I could hear more, I followed Rachel to the linen closet in the dining room. She swung the door open. All the expensive linens and tablecloths sat neatly pressed and ready for service on the shelves. I reached past Rachel to the top shelf for the thick photo albums only Iris had the patience to fill.

Once down, we took the armload back to Iris' room after motioning for Kory to come join us. Rachel didn't say it, but it was clear she didn't want Aiden figuring out what we were doing at the house.

Back on the bed, we each grabbed an album and started poring over the photographs.

After a few moments, Kory asked, "Mom, what exactly are we looking for?"

Rachel, hunched over an album, answered, "Look in the background, foreground, anywhere that might look off. Pay special attention to water and Iris' face."

Knowing that was a vague answer, I started scanning each beach picture. A bit of sadness stirred as I studied each one remembering all the times I spent with Iris. All the stories she told us and the memories of our adventures. I always thought it was we who kept her young, but now I knew it was her power that kept her up to par with two little girls who didn't know the meaning of slow down and rest.

The pictures were snapshots of the three of us building castles in the sand, laying on the beach, and my favorite, finding all the weird seashells and other things from the ocean. I stifled a laugh. Now, I knew why all those young men volunteered to take pictures for Iris. She must have oozed Siren-ish allure.

"Here we go," Rachel said, holding a picture out for us. I recognized the photo from two summers ago, taken by a cute boy Kory met who was on vacation with his family. It was the three of us sitting on the beach with our toes in the water. The ocean was calm that day and the boy stood in the water off to the side. We were facing the camera, smiling with the excitement of the sun and surf.

"That's from two years ago. What's so remarkable about it?" Kory asked, squinting to see the hidden remarkableness.

Rachel pointed with her long index finger and perfectly polished nail. "First off, how many eighty- year-old women look like that without surgery?" She was right. Iris always looked young and that day was no exception. Certainly not twenty-something young, but not eighty, and maybe not even sixty.

Rachel continued, "Second, look at the water around the three of you. The water coming up and lapping into you." Kory and I both leaned in closer to see. The water was white where it hit us and glistened like glass. It was so bright, I could barely make out our feet.

I shook my head. "That glistening? That could be the sun reflecting off the water, Rachel."

Kory shrugged.

Rachel appeared exasperated. "It's not the sun reflecting off the water. It's your powers. All three of you. Anytime more than one Elemental is present, your abilities are stronger. Get three together?" She shook her head, her eyes wide. "You can bring down entire buildings while destroying a powerful demon if you're not careful."

With neither one of us convinced, Rachel rolled her eyes. "I think your abilities are surfacing now because a demon is in Webster Mills. I've felt the demon's presence at times, but I can't pinpoint it. The onslaught of visions and voices will only intensify until we find the man the demon possesses. The stronger the demon, the more power it will take to bring it down. It may take all three of us working together to destroy it." She moved off the bed towards the door. "Get some rest and we'll go down to the beach early in the morning. It's time you met someone."

CHAPTER EIGHTEEN

We didn't have anything other than canned food in the house to eat, so Rachel decided we should eat at Buffer's, a restaurant not too far from the house that serves amazing barbeque and shrimp burgers.

Aiden arranged for our flight at 1:30 the next afternoon, one day earlier than originally planned. Rachel told him that sounded great as she wanted to take us out early in the morning to the beach for some fun. When Aiden frowned, Rachel smoothed it over by telling him this was her old stomping ground and she didn't know when we would come back again. He nodded slowly and kissed her on the cheek.

Halfway through dinner, Aiden decided to tell us about a conversation he had earlier in the day with a few of the members regarding homeschooling. Before he could finish his triumphant story, I butted in and wiped the smile right off his face.

"Kory and I already told you we are not going to be homeschooled." I set my fork down.

Kory didn't say anything as we watched Aiden's face. The smile was definitely gone. However, as we were in a public place, he was not about to cause a scene. Aiden Blake did not work like that. Rachel frowned, but remained quiet.

Aiden kept his gaze on me steady while he ran his hand over his newly dark stubble, his elbow on the table. The bandage was gone and there appeared to be small cuts across his knuckles. His eyes shifted around and landed on me again. As he leaned forward, his chilling smile grew again.

"You'll do whatever I say as long as you are under my roof, Ava. And Kory has at least two more years *under my roof.*" He said the last three words slowly, punctuating each syllable. I looked from Rachel to Kory. Rachel was giving Aiden a "teenage girls will be teenage girls" look that made me want to stab her with my fork.

Kory paled. She was a pawn in a game between Aiden and me. I stayed only for Kory. She was the reason I hadn't come back to North Carolina for good.

I opened my mouth to tell Aiden what he could do with his roof when Kory touched my arm. She mouthed the word, "enough." I couldn't tell if she didn't want me to cause a ruckus in the restaurant or if she was tired of the bickering between Aiden and me.

"Hi, Brewer family!" Freya popped up next to me at the table. "When did you get in?" She asked as she smiled at Rachel and Aiden. I'd told her about Carey House, but nothing about the visions or our new-found powers.

Aiden smiled at Freya as he eyed us both. I could tell she was smitten. "It was a last-minute decision. Someone broke into the house here. And you are?" he asked. He placed his hand on Rachel's, who'd been quiet pretty much the entire meal.

Freya threw her hands up to her mouth in a shocked expression. "Oh, I'm sorry. I'm Freya Montgomery, Ava's friend. I saw you two at the funeral. Ava's told me so much about you, I felt like we'd already met."

"Hmm." I watched as Aiden nodded his head at her, his smile never wavered. Freya's father walked up to the table carrying a to-go box.

"Ava and Kory, so good to see you in town!" Mr. Montgomery said in his over-exuberant voice. Freya got his perky personality.

"Mr. Montgomery, this is our mother, Rachel Brewer and her fiancé, Aiden Blake," I said as I motioned to the couple with frozen smiles plastered on their faces. I could tell Aiden wanted to finish our conversation instead of meeting my friends. "Mr. Montgomery is the mayor of Locklyn," I added. To my amusement, Aiden's expression changed. Mr. Montgomery now had Aiden's full attention.

I watched as Aiden stood up and shook the man's hand. "Please, join us for dinner."

"Oh no, Freya and I just ran in to pick up our order. My wife is waiting in the car." Mr. Montgomery shifted the large box and patted Freya's arm to let her know it was time to leave.

Aiden sat back down and laced his fingers with Rachel's again. Oddly, Rachel still hadn't spoken. Suddenly, I felt warmth emanating from her. Not like the heat energy she demonstrated in the dining room at Carey House, but what other people might mistake as a slight warm breeze. Was she using her Elemental energy now?

"I would like to have a meeting with you tomorrow morning regarding a piece of commercial property located between Locklyn and Holden Beach." Aiden said slowly to Mr. Montgomery.

Freya's father stared at Aiden open-mouthed and then looked at Rachel. I watched as Rachel lifted her gaze to meet Freya's father's. It was undeniably flirtatious.

Aiden continued, "So, we have an appointment in the morning at City Hall?"

"Yes, of course, I can meet with you in the morning about commercial property. I look forward to it!" The man bellowed again before nodding at us and then turning on his heel and heading for the door.

Freya stayed behind a moment. She turned to me and put her hand up. "Okay, back up. You didn't tell me someone broke in." Freya's eyes bulged. I should have told her everything. Velma from the Scooby gang was Freya's spirit animal. She wouldn't rest until she found the culprit, but right now I didn't have time to fill her in. Something weird had just happened at our table with Aiden and Rachel and Freya's father.

"I just haven't had a chance to talk to you since then. We only found out about it last night and we're leaving tomorrow. Isn't your mom waiting on you in the car?" I asked quickly, trying to change the subject.

Freya eyed me suspiciously. She knew I was hiding something.

Come on, Freya. Don't bust me out. I'll tell you later. If only my Elemental slash Siren powers included telepathy.

"Yeah, I guess I'd better go. Call me later and let me know what's going on." I could only imagine the telepathic conversation we'd have right now.

I nodded my head at her as she waved goodbye to Kory. I couldn't help but notice the amused smile on Aiden's face. What was that about? Three minutes ago, he struggled not to rip my head off. Now he was smiling that stupid charming smile at my best friend.

The Blake-Brewer table ate their remaining dinner in silence.

~ ~ ~

I was still fuming when we got home. There was simply no way I was going to spend my senior year home schooled by the members of the Order of Greatness. Nothing wrong with homeschooling, but in this case, it's the instructors and their agenda. How could Rachel not see how controlling Aiden was? And what was with her using Elemental energy on Freya's father? For what reason? For Aiden?

We stopped at the grocery store on the way home for a half gallon of milk, fruit, eggs, and Poptarts. After changing into a pair of shorts, I went into the kitchen and put on a pot of coffee, hoping it would help me relax enough to forget about this evening's argument. While the coffee was brewing, Aiden walked in as if right on cue.

"I thought I smelled some great coffee making." He sounded cheerful and it amazed me how quickly his temper could turn on and off. Always ready with that smile. He got down a mug from the cabinet since I already had mine ready, and stood, leaning against the counter opposite me with his arms folded. I realized Aiden was staring at my legs and I felt a warm sensation followed by dread. Maybe this was what Kory meant when she said she felt uncomfortable around Aiden.

I turned and faced the coffee pot because I wasn't sure what else to say or do. Was I jumping to conclusions? Was Aiden a charming, but lecherous man? As if hearing my thoughts, Aiden came over and stood facing me, his hip against the counter. He was so close I could smell his designer cologne.

"A watched pot doesn't finish any faster." He said in a conspiratorial tone. When I didn't respond, he added, "Your friend Freya seems nice."

"She is. We've been friends since the sixth grade. I'm surprised you could get an appointment with the Mayor so quickly. He's a very busy man."

Aiden shrugged. "Well, maybe you can invite Freya to visit Carey House this summer before school starts."

I cocked my head as a thought crossed my mind. It was probably the stupidest plan I could ever think of and if it didn't work, Aiden would think there was something wrong with me. But, now was as good a time as any.

I placed both hands on the edge of the counter. I wasn't entirely sure what I was doing but decided to let intuition take over. "I need some coffee to think with a clear head." I said, eyeing him steadily. His eyes locked with mine and he leaned closer, studying my face.

I continued, "Kory and I don't want to be homeschooled. It's not for the best, not for us." I spoke slowly and when I was finished speaking, I waited. Aiden narrowed his eyes, and for a moment, my insides dropped to a panic, but I didn't let it show on my face or in my eyes. This was the same tone of voice I'd heard Rachel use on Aiden before. My insides swirled as the heat intensified. Could I catch fire? Was this worth it? I really, really needed Aiden to change his mind. I kept that thought on repeat.

The coffeemaker beeped, and Aiden leaned back, still staring at me. "Hmm. I think you're right, Ava. You and your sister are smart and don't seem to fall for outside influences. Peer pressure has never been a problem for you, I bet." He reached over and with one finger snapped my charm bracelet playfully, a smirk spread across his lips.

I poured mine and his coffee as calmly as I could, praying my hands wouldn't shake.

Aiden continued, "Alright. Starting in the Fall, you can go to public school." He reached down with one hand, grabbed his cup while simultaneously kissing the side of my head. "Thanks for the coffee."

I shut my eyes when he left the kitchen and breathed out the panic-stricken breath I'd been holding in. I didn't know if I'd used my power or somehow conned Aiden into letting us stay in public school.

Either way, there might be Hell to pay later.

CHAPTER NINETEEN

We only had a few hours before we would leave for the airport, so we got up early to make our jaunt to the beach with Rachel. While getting dressed, I pulled Kory into the bathroom and shut the door firmly behind me, slipping the little scroll from the Meeting room into my shorts pocket.

"I think I got Aiden to let us go to public school in West Virginia." I whispered to her, since I wasn't sure if Rachel would be angry if she knew what I had done. Or, if she had some sort of supernatural hearing that worked through walls.

"What? How? He was pretty determined last night. Even Mom agreed with him it would be for the best." Kory pulled her long dark hair up into a bun.

"I think I used our powers on him."

Kory turned and stared at me. "What do you mean? You didn't..." her voice trailed off as her eyes grew wide.

"No! Of course not!" I had to force myself to keep my voice down. "I looked at him the way Rachel does and told him it wasn't a good idea. I got scared, but it worked. I could feel this energy inside of me bubbling up. Kind of like when you love someone, or you really want something."

"Oh, the way I wanted that new Coach bag last Fall."

"Umm, yeah, but on a deeper level," I rolled my eyes.

"I know what you mean. I'm just messing with you." She turned back around to face the mirror.

"I can't say for sure it's what changed his mind, but afterwards, I don't think I have ever felt so powerful. Or, scared."

"Are you insane, Ava? You know we can't play with that fire or something bad could happen," she said, watching my reflection in the mirror while she applied eyeliner.

"I know, but if I hadn't he was going to make us homeschool with those people who would try to brainwash us into their cult or whatever it is. Anyway, I think we have been using a tad bit of the power for a while now and didn't know it. Think about it. Jake Henderson in Webster Mills. The boys here. Dillon. Getting them to do things we needed done. You think they did that out of the goodness of their hearts?" I laughed.

Kory didn't. My younger sister turned to face me with the familiar expression Iris used when she doled out advice.

"And what happens if one of these boys, or a man, wants more than just a smile and a pat, Ava? Are you prepared for that? I'm not. Mom needs to teach us how to protect ourselves," Kory turned back to the mirror. "Plus, you know she knows how. What she did in the dining room with the heat?"

It was true. Rachel's power was more than glittering water.

A knock came to the bathroom door. I opened it just a crack. Rachel stood against the doorframe, her hair still wet from a shower. She had on a pair of shorts and a long cable knit sweater.

"We need to go now. Are you wearing your suits?" If she meant our bikinis, then yes. Obviously, she had her swimsuit on under her clothes. Kory pushed me aside and opened the door.

"We're ready," Kory said.

~ ~ ~

Aiden had plans to meet a few people in Locklyn, including the Mayor, this morning about property and needed the rental car, so we took Iris' Buick. The drive to the beach wasn't far and Rachel parked at a public beach access. This particular area was more residential than tourist, so it was vacant this morning and I closed my eyes, savoring every second.

The familiar roar of the waves as they washed ashore. The smell of salt and sand. My skin started to grow moist from the salt in the air. I loved it here. It had felt like home from the moment Iris brought us for mini vacations or as a special treat on a hot day.

Rachel whispered in my ear, "Come on."

We followed Rachel past dunes and around rocks. We were at the end of the beach which meant fewer houses and a smaller likelihood that residents would see us. She stopped on the beach and shed her shorts and sweater. Kory and I followed suit since we weren't sure what Rachel planned.

The three of us stepped into the water only a few inches deep. At once I could feel my feet sink into the sand, so I had to shift quite a bit. Rachel removed a necklace from around her neck and held it up. Kory frowned at me. I couldn't tell if it was because we all knew not to wear any jewelry down to the ocean since it could get lost and the saltwater is corrosive, or if it was because Rachel resembled a model getting ready to make a sacrifice. I scanned the area for onlookers but didn't see anyone.

I suddenly recognized the necklace Rachel held high in the air. It was Iris'. It was the only piece she would wear to the beach since it consisted of shells and quartz. Rachel held it above her head and whispered something I couldn't hear over the sound of the waves. After a long moment, she turned to us and handed me the necklace.

"I need you to hold this above your head and say, 'From the depths below and the sky above, bring me the one to train the young.' Say it three times, and then give the necklace to your sister. Kory, you do the same thing." When I hesitated, Rachel said she would say it with me.

I held the necklace high like Rachel had and took a deep breath, then said the words three times. Kory did the same. When Kory finished, she handed the necklace back to Rachel. Rachel held her hand up with it wrapped around her wrist.

We waited.

I wasn't sure what to expect. Everything looked the same. Would a Leviathan appear out of the water? A Krakken emerge from the sea?

Rachel frowned, clearly exasperated. Just when I started to feel stupid, I heard a whisper on the water above the ocean waves.

At first it was soft almost inaudible. It rose above the waves and onto the shore becoming louder and louder.

"Rachel."

"It's Rachel."

"Our Rachel."

The whispering grew louder and surrounded us. I shivered but held fast when I saw Rachel hadn't moved. She smiled an I-told-you-so grin. I followed her gaze out into the ocean and saw him.

All I could do was stare. There, coming out of the waves, was a man. Not just any man, but a man whose body was artistically chiseled from a piece of marble. As he walked closer, I could see the ripples of muscle on his abs and arms. Everything about him radiated perfect. The early morning sun glistened off the beads of water on his tanned skin and dark hair. As strange as all of this was, I wasn't surprised that he wore a pair of jeans, of all things.

I couldn't take my eyes off him to look at Kory. Still, closer he came, watching the three of us standing just a few feet now in the water.

When he was only an arm's length away, he stopped and regarded us individually. I thought my heart might stop when his eyes bore into mine and I literally felt his gaze survey my body.

"Rachel, you summoned me with two Elementals in tow? Where is Iris?" His voice was deep.

Rachel's voice was raspy when she answered him. "Forgive me. Iris passed away." At the mention of Iris' passing, the man looked genuinely sad. He placed one hand in his pocket.

"These are my daughters, Ava Grace and Kory Ann." Rachel's eyes lowered in obvious respect.

The man's jaw clenched as he regarded Kory and me again. Up close he looked to be in his twenties, not yet thirty.

Then he spoke directly to Rachel.

"Is there a demon here? Is that why you have called me?"

Rachel nodded. "There is, I believe in West Virginia, but I don't know who yet. Ava and Kory need trained in their powers. Whatever this demon is, it's strong and has somehow veiled its location. I am afraid it's going to take all three of us to find and destroy it."

"The power of three. These girls are young, Rachel." He stepped behind us. I could smell the saltwater on his skin as he came close. When his hand touched my hair, I turned my head and gazed into his gorgeous green eyes. He was studying me as if trying to reach into my mind and see if I was worthy.

Or ready.

"Calder, we haven't much time. We have to leave soon. Will you help me?" Rachel came over and stood beside him. Calder still held a ringlet of my hair in his hand.

He seemed to ignore Rachel's plea. "You know, I loved Iris very much. The news of her death saddens me. She told me she was sick the last time she was here. She told me you would come. I held her in my arms for a long time…" his voice trailed off. He dropped his hand from my hair and looked away for a brief moment towards the ocean. The wind picked up and a lock of Rachel's blond hair swirled around Calder's massive bicep.

"The cave on the other end of the island; I will meet you there."

CHAPTER TWENTY

As Calder walked back out into the sea, we grabbed our clothes and rushed to the car to drive to the opposite end of the island to the caves. The island authorities didn't allow anyone to go into the caves. Rumor was that the tide at times would fill the cave with water and you could drown if you got stuck in there. There were urban legends of children dying that way. We didn't know if it was true or not but had never attempted to try our luck.

As Rachel drove, Kory and I started barraging her with questions. Who was he? How did he just appear? *What was going on?*

Rachel spoke fast as it didn't take very long to reach the caves on the small island. "The legend about Sirens state they were creatures who lured sailors, right? And I told you we only look for and destroy demons. God created our particular branch of Elementals to lure men possessed with the demon to destroy it. These women were beautiful, clever, alluring, and empowered, even if they never felt they were before. Knowing what a threat these women posed, throughout time the demons have perverted the stories about them, making the Sirens, and thus Elementals like us, monsters."

She continued, "Calder is here to help guide the Elementals in each generation. It's not just our family either. There are others on the east and west coasts, as well as other continents. Calder is there for them all, but you can only summon him, and he isn't omnipotent. One place at one time."

Rachel made a right turn onto the street leaving the residential area behind. Kory spoke, grabbing the back of my seat and pulling herself up, so her head was between our seats. "So, Calder and Iris had a thing? Is that why she never married?"

"That's all you got out of that?" I pretended Kory's audacity floored me, but secretly I wanted to know.

"He was the reason Iris never married, but it wasn't a thing. She didn't need to marry because she could sense when he was here. She never had to summon him. Calder doesn't age. He is immortal, but he can't leave the coast and come very far inland. His power diminishes greatly if he does." Rachel slowed down to find a safe parking spot where she could hide the car in case someone drove by.

Kory sat back in her seat. "This is like a fairy tale. It's so romantic. Go Iris!"

Rachel turned off the engine and swiveled to look at Kory. "No, not romantic. Tragic. Didn't you hear him? He knew she was dying the last time she was here. He watched her age. Our power can only keep your health up for so long, even when you are good to yourself. Calder must remain in the ocean and watch over the others. It's both a blessing and a curse."

Calder was already deep in the cave when we got there. He was sitting on a rock ledge over a pool of water. I stepped carefully since the water made the rocks slick. This part of the cave was huge with both stalagmites and stalactites everywhere. I wondered if the rumors were true about the cave filling with water. It was large enough to fit a small home. If it did fill with water quickly, there would be no way to get out fast enough.

Rachel stopped to wrap her beach towel around her suit tightly again. Calder jumped down from the ledge to help her step up. When he reached for me, I held his gaze. He had the face of an angel.

As I took his hand, he wrapped his fingers in mine. Suddenly, my insides twisted. I crouched on the rock where I stood, preparing for the full onslaught of a vision. Instead, my gut filled with enormous sadness, heart wrenching sadness and I felt my chest to see if I had a hole where my heart should be. It became unbearable and I placed my forehead on the cool rock. The sound coming out of my mouth was pure and utter grief. I squeezed my eyes shut as I slipped into darkness.

I wasn't sure if I was dreaming or not, but I found myself floating along the shore in broad daylight. I tried to move my arms in front of me as I rose and fell with the wind, but all I could see was mist. Somehow, I was the mist.

I moved silently along the beach and up a little rock cliff at the end of the island that overlooked the ocean. The wind propelled me towards a couple sitting near the cliff's edge. The man sat with his legs stretched out in front of him and his arms wrapped around a woman as they surveyed the ocean. I floated closer to them. I knew them.

Calder and Iris.

I strained to come closer, to hear Iris, to see her startling blue eyes again. I hovered right in front of them, but neither took notice of me. Iris ran her delicate hand over Calder's wrist and up his arm. He pulled her closer and kissed her temple.

She turned her head as she caressed the side of his face with the palm of her hand. It was such an intimate gesture, much deeper than a kiss.

"Calder, I'm sick," Iris said.

Calder pulled her even closer to his bare chest and Iris let her head drop to her shoulder. "Soon, I won't be able to come here anymore. The girls don't know who they are and Rachel...I have to call Rachel."

The heartache in Iris' voice was palatable.

"Shhh, Iris. I promise you, I will do all I can for them when they come." Calder narrowed his eyes at the ocean as his jaw clenched. He was holding back so as not to upset her.

Iris reached into the pocket of her blue maxi dress and produced a rock. I moved in closer to see as the sunlight gleamed off the object. Not a rock. She held a large blue quartz stone up to Calder's face.

"I empowered this to help link you to Ava. She is the older one, smart and clever. I feel she is the strongest of the three and will need your help. Something is coming, and I won't be here to guide my girls. This will help."

As Calder took the quartz and squeezed it in his hand, it broke into three equal pieces. Iris began to cry. In all my life, I'd never seen her cry. My beautiful, caring, sensible guardian was like a small child. Iris took a piece of the stone and put it back into her pocket. Calder slipped the other two stones into his pocket and turned Iris sideways onto his lap. He buried his face in her blonde hair as he wrapped his strong arms around her fragile body.

I didn't want to see anymore.

~ ~ ~

I woke up to Calder holding me in his arms on the cave floor. His green eyes shone. It was his his grief for Iris that I felt. Although he made no sound, I could see it in his eyes. I placed my hand on his wet chest. His skin felt hot as his chest rose and fell with every breath. Iris connected Calder and me in all of this with a quartz stone. As if sensing my realization, he pulled the blue stones from his pocket and showed them to me, and then slid them back.

I understood. He carried his memories of Iris with him.

Kory dropped to her knees beside us as Calder pushed my hair away from my face.

"Iris' girls," he breathed and shook his head.

Never had I wanted a man to kiss me before like I suddenly wished Calder would. Apparently, Iris' link between us was strong. Seeming to sense this thought, Calder smiled. When the pain subsided, he helped me up and we followed him to the ledge above the pool of water. I could only feel a resonating sadness.

Rachel stood beside me and mouthed the words "You, okay?" When I nodded, she continued around to the other side of Calder as he began to speak.

"Your powers are already inside of you, only not focused and unrealized. God chose your lineage to hunt down demons hell-bent on destroying humanity. Many of these demons possess lustful men. Your powers attract both the human man and the possessed. Do not feel sorry for these possessed men. They followed their own desires knowing better and thought it would never catch up with them. They spit in the very face of God. This allows a demon full entry into their bodies. Right now, you see and hear past and present demons in the bodies they possessed. These visions become stronger the closer a demon is coming. Evil begets evil and attracts its own."

"The next time a vision is coming over you, force it away. Remind it that it has already seen defeat. But pay close attention, the stronger the vision, the stronger the present demon has become. Together the three of you will be able to defeat a very powerful demon, but don't be fooled. It will try to trick you, and most importantly, try to separate you. You need to use all of your senses to subdue the demon. Your voice alone has great power. A song can lure the demon to you. Subconsciously, you already know how to lure in the demon and make him do what you want. I need to show you how to destroy him." Calder jumped into the pool of water and waved at Rachel to join him. She pulled her towel off and leapt into the water.

Once Rachel was in the water, Calder moved to the opposite side of the pool. "When the demon or even an apparition makes itself known, you need to focus all of your power into your core. Imagine your power like a ball of energy. In your mind, move that ball of energy to your core and let it build. Concentrate on extending the energy outwards, down your arms, and into your hands." The whole time he spoke, Calder demonstrated with his core and arms. I had to remind myself to focus on the lesson at hand and not on the Greek hero before me. Was it possible to have twelve pack abs?

"Anytime you are feeling weak, you need to get to water. Saltwater is best, but freshwater will work. Air, fire, and earth will give you some energy, but not like the ocean. You need to harness the element's power." He turned to face Rachel. "Alright, Rachel, I am the demon. Hit me."

Rachel smiled a devilish smile without ever showing her teeth. She continued to stare at Calder, but it wasn't a glare. It was bewitching. She looked like she wanted to eat him all up. Apparently, she and I shared the same food cravings. Unfortunately, it was the same grin I saw her give Mr. Montgomery last night.

Without warning she raised her arms and a flash came out of the palms of her hands aimed directly at Calder. The force hit him fully in the face and sparked the water around him. Kory and I grabbed each other and scrambled back from the edge of the rock so as not to get electrocuted.

When the sparks died down, I half expected to see Calder and Rachel floating in the water. But they were fine. Rachel climbed out of the pool of water scrunching her long blonde hair with her hands. Calder was still in the water. He looked even more alive.

"Come here, Kory Ann. It's your turn," he said. Kory looked at me.

"Well, I guess if I don't make it back you can have my iPad and Mac," she joked.

I half-laughed.

"Oh, stop worrying," Rachel said, pulling her sweater on. "Calder is not a demon, so he is immune to our powers. All of them." That last bit I wondered if she had said for my benefit. I hadn't dreamed of trying any luring business on Calder.

It took Kory much longer to throw a ball of energy at him.

"Why can't I get it?" Kory pouted in the water.

"You will. Your powers are only now surfacing. In three years, they will be at full strength. This means you need to focus hard. Now hit me." We waited while Kory stared Calder down. Nothing happened.

"Kory, honey," Rachel leaned over the rock ledge to the point I was afraid she would fall in, sweater and all. "Who do you like?"

"What?" Kory asked, never taking her eyes off Calder.

"Come on. What teenage boy do you think is really hot right now?"

Kory thought for a second. "My friend Dillon is kind of hot, I guess." Kory said. I rolled my eyes, but Rachel continued.

"Okay, think about Dillon right now. Calder is a demon who is going to attack you, but you need to clear your mind and think about what you would do to Dillon if he were here. I know it sounds silly but concentrate."

I watched as Kory's expression slowly changed from a frustrated frown to her mother's devilish grin. She shot two short bursts of energy across the pool to Calder. We clapped for Kory like a bunch of cheerleaders.

"Your turn, Ava," Calder said and reached up to help me into the water. When his hands touched mine, a spark ignited the water around us. If I didn't know better, I would have thought Calder had tricked me into a vat of boiling water, except it wasn't hot at all. The water bubbled and streaks of blue and red moved across the bottom.

"Ava is eighteen," Rachel said.

"That is only part of it."

When he didn't elaborate, I waded to the opposite side of the pool. The water was at a constant roll.

"Ava, hit me and try not to blow my head off." I made a face at him and half-heartedly raised my arms. The bursts of energy that streamed across the water were the longest and brightest thus far. After thirty seconds of this and no end in sight, Calder moved his hands and literally pulled the streams of energy into him.

"Enough," he said. I dropped my arms. The water ceased moving. No one clapped or cheered.

"I told you she's eighteen," Rachel whispered.

After about another hour of learning to focus our powers, and me spraying everyone with water, Rachel announced we needed to leave.

"Ava, wait. I want to talk to you," Calder touched my arm, sending goose bumps over my already chilled body. Rachel shot him a look but didn't argue. Kory and she trekked out to the car.

Alone in the cave with Calder probably should have felt uncomfortable but didn't. He sat down on a rock and placed his hands on his knees. He appeared trying hard to work a puzzle out in his mind. Not knowing what to say or do, I stood waiting and staring at him. He was magnificent, that was for sure. Every time he glanced in my direction, my heart fluttered. I observed the roundness of his shoulders and how those muscles met the others in his arms, hard and chiseled. The smallest movement showed the muscles working under the skin.

"Siren and most Elemental powers don't work on me."

"What?" Was I drooling?

"The look on your face. If you're trying to lure me, it won't work." Calder smiled, like he knew a secret.

"I'm not trying to work anything on you. I'm waiting to see what you wanted to talk about." I knew my answer came off a bit firm, but I had only been staring at the man.

He stopped smiling at my answer. "I kept you back because you're different than the others. Stronger, and I think, with more abilities. Your abilities are different than Rachel's or Kory Ann's. In fact, different from any of the others, including Iris," he said, with a sad smile.

I let his statements sink in. This was proof I really was an outsider now. Even an immortal man surrounded almost daily by Siren-like women thought so.

Calder moved off the rock to stand close to me. I didn't move away, only lifted my head to look into his eyes. He stood a good eight inches taller than me which made me strain all of my five-foot-six-inch body. What a time not to be wearing heels.

"My grief inside for Iris is enormous and you felt it. I think it's due to the stones she empowered." He pulled the stones from his pocket again.

I nodded my head. "I think so. She wore a piece of that quartz on a necklace. She'd made it herself. We buried her with it." I glanced up at the cave ceiling and silently commanded my tears not to fall. When I felt confident I wouldn't ugly cry, I continued, "Weird things have been happening to me since she died. I thought it was this power, but I feel I've known you forever. Somewhere in my mind I feel I know your secrets, your past, but I can't quite bring them to the surface."

Calder looked thoughtful for a moment.

"You should go. I'm going to see an old friend about this. The stone links us, but it shouldn't create such a strong connection. Your very energy feels like Iris. I don't know why your powers are different. I don't know why…" His voice trailed off. When he didn't say another word, but turned and faced the cave wall, I made my way to the entrance. As I walked out of the cave, I swore I heard him say "Iris."

But, it could have been the crashing of the waves on the rocks.

CHAPTER TWENTY-ONE

We arrived at the house in time to see Aiden and Dillon standing on the front porch talking.

"Dillon, what are you doing here?" Kory asked, clearly surprised at her suitor who'd returned to the scene of the crime.

"I came to see you, but your stepdad said you'd gone to the beach," he answered.

"Yes, imagine my surprise when Dillon happened to show up here during our impromptu trip," Aiden said, patting Dillon on the back. His eyes met mine. Did he know the truth about the window?

Rachel flew past Aiden and Dillon and headed for the front door. "Girls, I suggest you get dressed before our flight. Good-bye, Dillon," she said before she disappeared into the house. She may have come off a bit rude, but she knew there was a chance Dillon had ratted us out.

Kory smiled nervously up at Dillon as they walked out to the street to where his bike was parked. No doubt Kory was trying to find out what he'd told Aiden. I gave a sideways glance at him. Aiden still held his stony glare. This time directed at my sister. He had to know. I looked down at my flip-flops and pretended a paint chip on the wooden porch was of great concern. Kory popped up onto the porch and headed inside - an angry Aiden hot on her heels.

Rachel had told him we were going to the beach, but we ended up taking much longer than we planned with Calder, and Aiden was furious at our irresponsibility. Or, so he said. He followed Rachel to the bathroom as she went to clean up for the flight. Kory and I escaped to our rooms to get dressed. Never had I been so grateful for outside public showers as this morning.

After getting dressed, I grabbed my bags and charm bracelet. I slid the bracelet on my wrist in the kitchen before making a pot of coffee. I could hear the muffled voices of Aiden and Rachel, still coming from the bathroom. Kory tossed one of her bags onto the kitchen floor in front of the back door.

"What's he mad about anyway?" Kory asked, grabbing the last Pop Tart from the pantry. "He knew we were going to the beach."

"I don't know. It's not like we are going to miss our flight." The plane wouldn't leave for another three hours, giving us plenty of time to eat breakfast.

"What did Dillon say?" I whispered to her.

"Nothing really. He didn't give us up or anything. He said Aiden asked him how he knew we were in town and he told him he passed our street and saw a car and assumed. I don't know if Aiden bought it though. He seems pretty mad. And it can't be about the flight." She grabbed a bottle of water off the counter. "There is something weird. Dillon said Aiden exchanged cell phone numbers with him."

"Can you delete the call history with Dillon? If Aiden looks on your phone, he's going to see we called him."

Kory took her phone out of her back pocket and started swiping. "Even if he did, I would remind him that Dillon's my friend. My call history is full of calls to my friends here in Locklyn."

"I know, but let's cover our tracks anyway."

A hard bang on the wall in the kitchen made us jump. The bathroom was on the other side of that wall. Kory and I exchanged glances. I walked quietly out of the kitchen into the hall. At the bathroom door I could hear the shower running and whispering but couldn't make out the words.

I hesitated for a second, and then knocked softly twice. "Rachel?"

Aiden's voice boomed back through the door. "We're busy. Go get ready for the plane."

I hurriedly backed away from the door. When I got to the kitchen, I waved for Kory to come over to the far end of the room.

"I don't know what is going on. I can't tell if they are fighting or…not."

Kory scrunched up her face to match mine. Neither of us wanted to think of the 'not' portion of that statement. Was Rachel using her power to calm Aiden's anger? I stopped my thoughts from going any further.

As I made my first cup of coffee, my mind kept reeling back to this morning and Calder. I should have shown him the scroll with the symbols, but it was hard to think around him. I had never felt that way about a man before and I had dated a few boys.

As much as I didn't want to admit it, maybe Rachel had those same feelings for Aiden. He was a charmer and made sure Rachel didn't do without anything. But, there was something below the surface I couldn't figure out.

Something not right. Something evil.

How could one person change so many people and get them to do whatever he wanted without having some form of power? And how much power did he hold over Rachel? He was charismatic, but was that all?

When Rachel and Aiden finally joined us in the kitchen all seemed well between them. Rachel was in a good mood which she was not when Aiden had greeted her at the door. Aiden acted as if he would buy Rachel the world, and I wondered again if she had used her power on him. Aiden leaned against the stove with his cup of coffee, his legs crossed in front of him, watching Kory and me. We were trying to empty the refrigerator of anything that would go bad before we left, mostly to keep our minds off what Aiden and Rachel may have done in our bathroom.

"Kory, where is your bracelet?" Aiden asked.

Kory turned towards him and placed her hand over top of her right wrist where the bracelet should have been. "Oh, I think I've already packed it."

Before Aiden took another sip of his coffee, he stopped with a dead stare. It was strange as his eyes were ice cold, but he was smiling.

"Don't you think you should go get it? I chose those bracelets for the three of you because you're my girls. I would appreciate it if you would make an effort to wear it."

Kory shrugged. She was shaking her head as she left the kitchen to fetch her other bag.

Rachel, who had decided to eat the last of the fruit, walked over and snuggled in Aiden's arms, forcing him to set his cup down.

"Aiden, I think it is wonderful that you bought these bracelets, I really do. But you make them sound like they're some sort of house arrest ankle bracelets. Lighten up a bit, honey. We can't wear them to the beach." She kissed him on the cheek, and then hugged him tightly.

Aiden held Rachel in his arms and continued watching me as he kissed the top of her head. I felt a cold tingle run up my spine.

CHAPTER TWENTY-TWO

The flight back to West Virginia didn't seem to take as long, maybe because I sat next to Kory while Aiden sat across the aisle. Throughout much of the flight, I peered out the window at the blanket of clouds. They appeared more like snow covered hills than mists of fluff. As I chewed my gum to help my ears pop, I wondered what Rachel saw in Aiden. Yes, he was rich and smart, but surely, she wasn't going to marry him for those reasons. Was it because she credited him with her ability to get clean?

Even with all of these new revelations – Elemental powers, demons, possessed men, Calder – I still didn't know if I could trust Rachel, let alone forgive her for placing her addiction first and giving us away to Iris. I still wanted to ask her about Freya's father, but trying to get her alone was almost impossible.

Aiden was manipulative, but people fawned all over him. As much as I didn't want to admit it, he and I might be a little alike. Hadn't I manipulated him in the kitchen to get him to change his mind about forcing us to homeschool with members of the Order of Greatness?

I made a face at my reflection in the window. I was nothing like Aiden.

Roger was waiting for us outside the airport to drive us back to Carey House. The two men began talking about the upcoming meeting as soon as the car pulled onto the road. Rachel and Kory were engrossed in a discussion about the recent sale at Victoria's Secret.

"Ava, do you want to go?" Rachel asked me. She was sitting in the middle of the backseat between Kory and me. "I can also make an appointment for the three of us for mani-pedis at Posh Lashes and Nails."

I looked down at the chipped nail polish on my fingers. I wanted to get back to my room and think about everything that had happened and try to decipher the symbols on the scroll again on my own.

"To the mall? Not this time. I'm kind of tired," I lied.

Aiden, who was sitting in the passenger front seat, turned to look at me and smiled. I couldn't see his eyes through his sunglasses, but I suddenly felt self-conscious. I reached for my phone in my handbag to keep from looking in his direction. Last night when I persuaded Aiden to allow us to attend public school, had I unintentionally led him on? Did he think I wanted to bribe him with "favors"? I shuddered. I swiped my phone to see two texts from Freya.

Text number one: **Saw your soon-to-be-stepdaddy in town today at the old rec center. Say what you will, but he looks GOOD. He said I can come visit you anytime I want. That he would fly me there!**

I rolled my eyes. Of course, he did. He probably would try to talk her into joining the Order too.

Text number two: **Btw, I asked/tortured Dillon into telling me he broke your window. He said Kory asked him to do it. WHAT IS GOING ON?**

I would definitely have to call her now before she told someone. Not that she would bust me out on purpose, but you never knew about well-intentioned adults. All it would take was for Freya to mention it to one of her parents and they would probably call Aiden. I deleted both texts.

"Were you able to seal any real estate deals while you were there?" Roger's question to Aiden pulled me from my trance.

"I made some headway. A couple of commercial properties look promising as well as a large but older auditorium-type structure that's housed in a secluded area. We could use them for meetings, workshops, clinics. Although the secluded area is perfect for a larger building and I think the house would make a fine shelter for members attending current programs."

"What house?" I asked, despite my resolve not to speak too much to Aiden.

He turned his head, "Iris' house."

"You can't let people stay in Iris' house. That's our home," I said, my voice beginning to rise.

"Why not?" He asked. "You aren't staying there, and you removed all the valuables. We haven't expanded to North Carolina yet and the house is in a great location for both residents and tourists who want to learn more about the Order. The Order's ability to help people realize their full potential even has Mr. Michaels interested."

"Mr. Michaels?" I asked, my voice sounding weak now.

Aiden turned further in his seat to get a better view of the three of us. Rachel and Kory said nothing. Did Rachel know the Order was buying up properties and expanding their influence in North Carolina and our small town?

"Members of the Order will take better care of the house than the caretaker I hired. Carey House is your home now." He looked at me. "If for some reason, you decide to leave, then you can resume staying in the house in your old room. I'll make sure the members only use the other two bedrooms."

Aiden resumed talking with Roger, but my mind was a million miles away. Kory was staring hard at her phone in her lap, but I could see she wasn't texting a friend or scrolling one of her several social media accounts.

Rachel didn't look at me at all.

Roger drove us right up to the door of Carey House and helped us remove our bags from the car. Martha came out to take our carry-on bags inside which gave me a chance to pull Kory away from Aiden and Rachel. Martha was a plump little woman, her gray hair knotted into a low bun. I'd spoken to her on several occasions, but mostly in passing. Today was no different as she hurriedly gathered our bags.

"Come with me to the greenhouse," I commanded in my sternest voice to my sister.

Realizing I meant business, Kory didn't question me, but walked with me quickly away from the front of the house. We stopped half way down the path to the greenhouse when we spotted Jake and another member working on the landscape. Didn't these people ever take a day off?

"We can't let the Order take over Iris' house," I said.

Kory sighed. "I know you want me to side with you on this, but I think Aiden is right. We're not living there anymore, and at least the other members can keep an eye on it. No one will break in if people are staying there," she said.

"No one broke in to begin with, Kory!" I said, probably a little too loudly.

Kory shrugged. "Just let it go."

Before I could say more, Jake and the other member walked up. Dirt mixed with sweat streaked his arms and face. Apparently, he'd been hard at work on the grounds, most likely, the entire day. The girl looked to be in her twenties with a long black braid casually draped over her left shoulder.

"Hey, it's good to see you two back," he said, wiping his forehead with the back of his arm.

"Hey!" Kory said to Jake, a little too excited. She apparently wanted to change the subject. "I'm heading into the house. Mom and I are running to Victoria's Secret to hit up a sale," she smiled up at him, and without looking at me or the girl, began her jaunt back up the path.

"Working hard?" I asked, as I watched the muscles in his shoulder move as he half-waved goodbye to my sister's back. Different from Calder's, yet somehow still attractive.

"Roger called me this morning and asked if I could help get things ready for tomorrow night's meetin'. Supposed to be an important one. How was your vacation?"

I shrugged, "It wasn't a vacation. We had to check on the house in North Carolina."

"Sounds like a vacation to me," he quipped. "Anywhere close to the beach is a dream come true. By the way, this is D'Netta Moore. She's one of Aiden's favorite members." D'Netta elbowed Jake in the ribs before offering her hand to me.

"Hi, I'm Ava Brewer."

"I know," D'Netta said, as she shook my hand. "Aiden talks about you all the time."

"Well, we'd better get back to work before someone thinks we're slackin'," Jake said.

D'Netta started back towards the greenhouse with Jake when I reached out and touched his arm. He seemed surprised at my forwardness.

"Um, Jake," I said, keeping my voice low so D'Netta didn't hear as she walked away. "I wondered if you could meet with me tomorrow before the meeting. Maybe inside the greenhouse?"

"Why?"

"I want to ask you some questions regarding the Order and I feel like you would give me complete and honest answers that I might not hear from other members. I want your perspective since you're my age."

Jake's mouth formed a serious expression as he leaned in closer to me. I could smell the mulch mixed with his sweat. I hoped maybe I could trust him.

"Yeah, I think I'd like to ask you some questions too, Ava. What time?"

"The meeting starts at seven o'clock, so maybe six?" I asked.

Jake nodded, but didn't say more as Aiden came down the path towards the greenhouse.

"Jake, you're here late again today. How did they con you into working on the landscape?" Aiden asked. Jake smiled a mesmerizing smile that reminded me a little too much of Aiden.

"They called and said they needed help and I was willing and free."

"Good, and I see they kidnapped D'Netta, too." Aiden said. He took his sunglasses off and a small look passed between them as he motioned toward the girl shoveling the red mulch into a plantar.

He turned to me. "We should introduce the two of you. D'Netta is a big help in the Order and isn't much older than you." Aiden said, as he reached for my hand.

I turned to leave. "Thanks, but we've already met." I hoped Jake wouldn't tell Aiden I wanted to talk to him alone about the Order tomorrow evening.

I felt their eyes on me as I walked back to Carey House.

Rachel and Kory must have eaten at the mall because neither came home in time for dinner. I'd tried to call Freya three times, but she didn't answer her phone. I finally sent her a text to call me when she could. There was no way I could tell her everything through messaging. Thankfully, Aiden was in the Meeting room with Roger, Julia, and a few other Elders, so I grabbed a plate of food and a bottle of water and headed to my room. Before I could make it out of the kitchen, Martha ran into me.

"Oh, hi Martha. I thought everyone who wasn't in the Elder meeting had left," I said as I tried to maneuver around the plump woman.

She stood just inside the doorway, blocking my way into the dining room. "I spent the day cleaning bedrooms. I came in to get my purse, dear." She didn't move. Martha was born and bred in Ireland and her accent was much thicker than Aiden's. "Where's your family?"

"Rachel and Kory went to the mall," I smiled. The woman still didn't move from the doorway.

Martha suddenly appeared nervous as she reached for my arm. She motioned for me to follow her to the end of the kitchen near the pantry door. I set my plate of food down on the butcher block table and followed her, wondering what on earth was going through her mind.

"Ava, please don't tell anyone, but I worry about you and ye'r sister and ye'r mother. When you clean houses, people forget you're about and say things. I hear things," she whispered as she kept her eyes glued on the kitchen doorway.

"What kind of things?" I asked.

"Not everything is as you see in front of you," Martha said cryptically. "I know I sound like an old crazy woman, but there is another world around us that you can't see and sometimes things leach through. We believed in spirits back home, but people don't talk about'em here. Carey House is full of bad spirits that want nothing more than to do harm to you and ye'r family," Martha's eyes teared up as she pulled her handbag from the pantry and dug through it to produce a small clear wallet of pictures. She handed them to me. "I left my family, my grown children in Ireland to follow Aiden when they wouldn't join the Order of Greatness."

"Why did you follow Aiden here?"

"I'd known Aiden Blake all his life. Raised by his grandmother after the tragic deaths of his parents. A good boy, smart, clever. And, oh so charismatic. People have always listened to him. He's a born leader and what he says makes sense. But, he's also changed. He followed that old Lyle Carey in the Order. Old man Carey was revered, but he was also mean at times. He made people do things. Focused ambition on the wrong things can lead a man down a terrible path. A path of no return. The boy I knew is now a man of great power and authority, yet also great brutality." A tear ran down Martha's face, but she didn't attempt to wipe it away.

"It was a mistake on my part to join. The Order controls many things in this world and the next. They have money and influence and power. The likes I've never seen before anywhere."

I studied the two pictures of a young man and woman, probably in their thirties, smiling with their happy momma Martha sandwiched between them.

"Can't you call your son and daughter? Maybe they would let you stay with them if you went back to Ireland," I said as I handed the pictures back. She stuffed them into her purse.

"No, the Order would never let me do that. If I tried to leave..." she trailed off. Martha suddenly stood up straight, the streaks of tears drying on her cheeks. "I've to go now, dear. Please be careful," she said as she bolted out of the kitchen.

I stood in stunned silence as I tried to wrap my head around what Martha had said. The Order wouldn't let her leave or call her children? She was clearly afraid of someone and she believed in the supernatural realm. I picked up my plate and made my way upstairs, making a mental note to try to talk to her again tomorrow when she was perhaps less emotional. She'd made the Order sound like the mob, complete with possible hitmen. Was it more than just a cult? Was the Order also a crime organization? That would explain the real estate deals and expanding assets. Or, was that "business" a cover for the real deal – demonic influence and power? My head hurt thinking about it.

I slipped into my short set pajamas and dropped my rings and bracelet into the jewelry box before settling in the bed with my plate of food and laptop. I needed to figure out the symbols on the scroll since I'd failed to ask Calder.

After about an hour of no luck, I shut the computer and let out a sigh. Whatever the symbols meant, I couldn't find any mention of them. I flipped my journal open to the page with my copied script. But the word staring back at me wasn't my scribble.

One word on the page in large letters.

RUN.

Martha had said she'd spent the day cleaning bedrooms. Had she found my journal and saw the symbols? She was a member. She probably knew what they meant. Was she warning me to run? Of course, with all the members jaunting around the house on any given day, it could have been anyone. I started to crawl out of the bed with the empty plate in my hand, when I heard it.

Ava.

I froze on the bed, the plate balancing precariously in my hand. The whisper surrounded me and seemed to originate from inside my head, but it wasn't scary like before. Instead, it was familiar. I knew this voice.

Ava, come to the balcony.

I set the plate on the nightstand and moved towards the balcony. My heart beat rapidly as I opened the French doors and stepped out onto the concrete. As I leaned on the metal railing, I scanned the grounds.

Then, I saw movement. On the far side of the pond sat a man looking up at me.

Calder.

Not possible. Rachel said Calder couldn't come too far inland, and West Virginia definitely did not have beaches. Yet, I was pretty sure he was Calder.

Ava, come down here.

I quietly raced down the flights of marble stairs, taking care to stop before I rounded a corner in case someone was there. I wasn't sure if Kory and Rachel were back yet, but I didn't want to run into a member of the Order, or worse, Aiden.

I slipped through the front door and around to the side of the house, slowing down closer to the pond. Calder was sitting on the stone wall wearing jeans, boots, and a tight tee shirt. Where did he get his clothes? I decided I would have to ask him one day.

"Calder, what are you doing here?" I whispered loud enough for him to hear.

Calder shrugged. "I can come on land, although I'm not as powerful this far from the ocean. Don't you remember? When you were just a girl, I showed up at your house once. Iris had put you to bed, but you got back up. I didn't come back to the house after that."

Suddenly, the memory flooded my mind. It had happened not long after we'd moved in with Iris. She'd set regular bedtimes for us, but I would always get back up for one reason or another. That night, I'd found her on the back porch with a man as they cuddled on the chaise lounge. She'd rushed me back to bed and when I'd asked who the man was, she'd said, "Nevermind, you. Now stay in bed."

I sat down beside him on the wall. "But, how did you get here? And how could I hear your voice in my room?"

Calder ran a hand through his dark hair before answering me. "I have my ways. The fact that the blue stone links us helps me to transport quickly to you. However, yours is the only mind I can project my voice into."

"Did you find out more about the stone?"

"According to my friend, Iris imbued it with her energy, but she must have accidently trapped a piece of her soul inside. If I destroy the stone, it will set her free," he took a deep breath and let it out slowly as I watched the rise and fall of his chest. "But, I need the stone to stay connected to you while the three of you battle the demon."

"Iris is trapped in the stone?"

"Only a piece of Iris' soul is trapped. The rest of her is where she belongs with the Creator, but she is incomplete."

We sat quietly by the pond for a while. Iris inadvertently linked us to her soul and that's why I felt this deep connection to Calder, and he to me. It wasn't a real attraction between us, but the love between Calder and Iris. I started to ask Calder to tell me more about where Iris was when I remembered the scroll.

"I found a scroll in the Meeting room here with strange symbols on it. I can't find the meaning of the symbols, but maybe it has something to do with what is going on here or whatever demon may be nearby," I said.

"Where is it?"

"It's in my room under my laptop on the bed. I meant to show it to you before, but I got caught up with all of the training."

He nodded his head and spoke again.

"Perhaps you can give it to me before I leave. I brought something for you I think you might like and find useful," Calder said. "Place your hand in the water."

At once I did as I was told. The pond water was cool, and I hoped the koi wouldn't decide to nibble on my fingers. I dipped my hand a little deeper into the still water. Calder's eyes appeared as mirrors, reflecting the moonlight on the surface of the water. He calmly placed his hand in the pond. An electric shock traveled through my hand, up my arm, and into my shoulder as I tried to back away.

"Calder, what -" before I could finish my sentence, Calder covered my mouth with his. In that moment, I forgot he almost blew my shoulder out or that someone may see us by the pond. I forgot about Rachel and Aiden and the Order. I even forgot about Jake. At that moment, heaven and earth ceased to exist. As I kissed Calder back, it wasn't like kissing a stranger. I knew him, and he knew me.

In a flash, I realized he'd moved us up against the side of the house, out of view, without ever taking his mouth away from mine. My body was pinned against the cool stones, but I didn't mind. As I felt my skin grow hot, Calder suddenly pulled back. I felt woozy as I stared up at him, my hands on his arms. He removed the quartz stones from his pocket as they pulsated and glowed, with each beat, they glowed brighter. He closed his fist around the stones.

"Ava, I'm sorry. I shouldn't have kissed you. This connection with Iris has me thinking you are Iris at times. I apologize." He let go of me and took a step back.

I wanted to cry.

Abruptly, he put his hand up for me to be still. I listened hard but couldn't hear what he could apparently. Was someone coming?

"I'll check your room for the scroll. I have to go. Be careful, Ava," and with that he vanished from sight in the blink of an eye.

I fixed my pajama shirt and closed my eyes as I hummed trying to gain control of my breathing. I wanted so much for him to come back. I felt like I might burst inside.

"What are you doing out here?" It was Aiden. He was coming around the side of the house. Lost in my thoughts I had moved away from the hidden nook and into full view.

Ava, your powers are in full effect. Your humming has lured him closer. Do not make eye contact with him. Calder's voice penetrated my mind.

I stared at the ground as Aiden approached. He stopped just a few feet away; I could see his Sperry's in the freshly mowed grass.

"I said, what are you doing out here alone?"

"I wanted to see the pond," I answered and looked over in that direction. My voice sounded husky and foreign to me as if I had a nightly whiskey habit. In my mind's eye, I could still see Calder sitting on the stone wall, his eyes gleaming at me.

"You're here by yourself? Or…were you planning to meet Jake?"

Jake? The accusation caused me to look up at Aiden. I hadn't even thought of Jake.

Too late. Aiden studied my face and the look out of his eyes revealed a man who had made a discovery. I became keenly aware that I was still wearing my pajama short set. I looked away quickly but felt Aiden's gaze scan my body. I forced all feelings for Calder away before attempting to meet Aiden's eyes again. I needed to get control of myself.

Aiden walked over to the pond, sat down on the stone wall with his legs outstretched, and crossed his arms. "D' ya' like'em?" His accent thickened as goosebumps covered my arms. He'd asked the question with a tone I'd never heard from him before.

I hesitated. Had he seen anything? Did he know?

"Who?"

Aiden rolled his eyes. "Jake," then he added quietly, "Someone's got ya' all worked up."

I turned on my heel as I fought to slow my breathing. "I think it's time I go back inside now," I said slowly over my shoulder, half turning, hoping it came off as an answer to his ridiculous accusation.

"It's not a bad thing. I'm simply saying, Jake's a good kid, but he's still a kid." I watched as the Colin Farrell look-alike lowered his head and then raised his eyes just high enough to regard me. "You on the other hand are a lot like your mother... and it's going to take a real man..." he let his comment trail off as he ran his hand over the back of his neck, still studying me with a hungry look in his eyes.

Whoa.

Turning my back to him, I answered, "Good night, Aiden." I walked hurriedly to the house vowing to always stay in control of the power to lure men. Kory was right. What would I do if someone thought I wanted more? Could the physical energy be enough to protect me from a human monster?

When I got to my room, I locked all the doors, including the balcony, and climbed into bed. The scroll was gone from under my computer. I assumed Calder must have found it with no problem. No wonder I heard his voice. He was near enough to hear the exchange.

Aiden's remarks replayed in my mind in a tone I never wanted to hear again. A tone he probably reserved for Rachel - sweet, sexy, wanting.

And with an undercurrent of brutality.

CHAPTER TWENTY-THREE

A couple of hours later, my phone buzzed next to my ear, rousing me from a Calder-filled dream. Kory's whispered voice greeted me.

"Are you asleep?" She asked.

"I was. Where are you?"

"At your bedroom door. Let me in." I jumped out of bed as silently as I could and unlocked the door. Kory pushed the door open before I could turn the knob.

As she shut and locked the door, I climbed into bed. "What are you still doing up? When did you get back?"

"What are you doing in bed is the question."

She smiled and climbed into the bed with me, stretching out on the opposite side. "I overheard Aiden tell Mom you were on the lawn by the pond tonight in your pajamas. He thought you were meeting Jake."

When I rolled my eyes, she pressed further. "So, were you meeting Jake?"

"I didn't meet Jake nor was I supposed to," I paused for a moment. Should I tell Kory about Calder? I wasn't ready to tell her about the scroll yet, especially since Calder had taken it to learn more.

"Well, before you tell me what happened – and you will tell me – I need to tell you about our demon-hunting adventure at the mall," she said, her eyes wide.

"What?!"

"We were at the store going through the racks when Mom said she felt something and asked if I felt it too, but I didn't. She said there was a demon nearby and maybe the one we're looking for, so she started humming this really strange tune. It was kind of a cross between a television show theme song and a lullaby. Anyway, we went to check out and a man came over and started talking to her. You'd a thought I wasn't even there!" Kory said, clearly an unimaginable thought.

She continued. "The man was flirting with her. I don't know if he was supposed to be there shopping or if he wandered into the store, but she talked to him in a low voice. So low at times I couldn't make out her words. After we checked out, we left the store, but the man followed us to the parking garage. I asked her if we should call for help, but she said she knew what she was doing. When we got to the car, Mom had me get in and shut the door. Then she turned and faced him," Kory's eyes were bulging by this point. As were probably mine.

"I watched through the window as he reached for her and she took one hand and sent an energy blast into his chest. It was so quick. If I hadn't been watching I would've missed it. The man fell backwards unconscious, but nothing happened. No demon appeared. Mom said he wasn't possessed, at least not yet. But, he had enough lust in him to answer her when she hummed."

I turned over to stare at the ceiling. Rachel's humming had lured some weirdo to her in the store. A pervert who wasn't even possessed. I certainly couldn't tell Kory I'd lured Aiden the same way tonight by accident. Not even my journal should know about that awkward – and possibly dangerous – situation.

"That sounds pretty scary. Are you okay?" I asked her.

"Me? Oh, I'm fine. It was almost like hands-on job experience," she said and laughed. "So, what happened with you tonight?"

"If I tell you, you can't tell Rachel or anyone else," I said, turning to face her. She still wore her heavy eye makeup from the day, and with her wild bed head look, she was close to resembling something out of a bad eighties music video. But, her face read that she would rather go to the guillotine than betray my trust. I sighed, "I met Calder tonight by the pond."

"Calder? I thought he couldn't come here."

"I did, too. Apparently, he can, but he's not as powerful here as he is closer to the ocean. He probably wanted to meet me at the pond to use the water as a resource."

"A resource for what?" Kory asked.

"I'm not sure. He said he brought something for me, but something strange happened, and then he kissed me."

Kory's mouth flew open so wide, I couldn't help but giggle - which made her giggle.

"Don't look at me like that," I said. "Somehow Iris linked Calder and me together. Sometimes what he felt for Iris leaches through."

"So, he thinks you're Iris at times?"

"I guess. It doesn't matter. Aiden showed up."

Kory's face went serious. "Did he see Calder?"

"No, Calder heard him coming and disappeared."

Kory seemed to ponder this and flipped onto her back, staring up at my ceiling fan.

I wanted to tell her about the strange symbols on the scroll, but I needed to give Calder time to decipher them, if he could. Just as I closed my eyes to welcome sleep, Kory rolled towards me.

"So, you don't know what Calder gave you? What strange thing happened at the pond before he kissed you?"

"I placed my hand in the water and he sent an electrical current through the water into my arm. It felt like I touched an electric eel." I automatically rubbed my left shoulder.

"And you haven't tried to use any Elemental energy from that arm since?"

"I haven't needed to try." I thought of Aiden and his remarks and turned my head, so Kory wouldn't question the disgusted look on my face. She didn't need to know about that exchange.

"Let's try it."

Before I could protest, Kory jumped out of the bed and pulled me with her. I smacked her hands trying to get away from her, but she was younger and, obviously, demented. She grabbed my wrist with both hands and pulled. I toppled to the floor. Kory laughed hard as she plopped down on the floor with me. We both hid our faces to keep from laughing hysterically out loud. That would surely get Aiden and Rachel up.

When I could finally breathe again, and with tears running down my cheeks, I choked out the question, "What are you doing?"

Kory's eye makeup had run even more and now her cheeks wore streaks of black kohl, giving her the appearance of a woman recently committed to the local asylum. She wiped her face with the back of her hand, and then onto her pajama pants. She was still giggling to herself.

"I want to try something." She crawled over to the balcony doors and dramatically reached for the door handle, acting like the girl from *The Grudge*. Again, we both buried our faces and laughed hysterically.

It took several minutes before we were both able to stand on the balcony without crying out in muffled laughter.

"Okay, which arm did Calder electrocute?" Kory asked.

I giggled again. Was there no end to this crazy giggling spasm? I held up my left arm.

"I'd better aim for something small, so no one notices" I said, trying to conjure the energy into my core.

"Wait!" Kory ran back into my room. She emerged carrying my coconut candle from Bath and Body Works along with its little lighter. She lit the candle and held it up.

"Here, I think you may need to use the fire as a resource since we don't have water."

I shrugged. "We have the water in the pond below. Maybe I can channel both."

"How about a tree in that far corner lot? No one will know if one falls," Kory said, pointing past the pond toward the edge of the forest.

Why not? I leveled my gaze over at the trees in the far distance and slowly focused on just one tree. One tree a little further than the other trees in that far lot. A tree not too large to be old, but not too thin for a sapling. I cleared my mind and concentrated on snapping the trunk in two. I felt a small spark in my core as the flame on the candle burned brighter, so I focused harder tuning everything out, including Kory. I thought about the tree, but also in my mind's eye, I remembered Calder's kiss just a few hours ago below this balcony on the ground. I thought about the great love he felt for Iris. The water in the pond bubbled with streaks of blue.

My core and chest burned now, and I raised my arms. A burst of red energy streamed across the estate, past the pond, towards the corner lot of trees. Except it didn't hit just the one tree. The energy sliced through the entire corner lot of trees, pulling them towards the house and tearing them all down. I dropped my arms.

More than ten trees lay on the freshly mowed lawn.

CHAPTER TWENTY-FOUR

The next morning, I watched as Aiden, Roger, and a few members rode ATVs out to the edge of the forest to examine the fallen trees from that parcel of land. The trees were not in the forest where they belonged. The Elemental energy had pulled their broken trunks and roots at least forty feet onto the cleared landscape.

I stood inside the balcony door, so Aiden and the others wouldn't see me. If Rachel figured out it was me, she would be furious. She hadn't told us not to practice but calling attention to three Elementals was probably frowned upon in the supernatural realm.

I peeked outside again at the group huddled at the trees, probably trying to figure out a way to move them off the property before the meeting tonight. If this group constituted the majority of people here this morning, then now might be the only opportunity I had to check out Aiden's office.

I took another peek before heading downstairs.

The second floor was quiet with the exception of Kory talking on her phone in the den. I passed by the door without stopping. If caught, I would rather take the blame than involve her. Plus, it sounded like she was having an engrossing conversation with one of her friends about a Netflix Original series.

The first floor proved a little trickier as members tended to walk through the Great Hall on a regular basis. I made my way down to the bottom marble step and sat down. After five minutes of not a single member making an appearance, including the ever-present Martha, I moved across the hall to the smaller hallway. The hall was narrow and Aiden's office door was directly across from the Meeting Room.

I placed my hands on the door. I would need to be careful. If last night proved anything, it was that I don't know how to control my power. I breathed deeply as I tried to will the energy to form in my gut. It was taking longer to form than before. Had I somehow tapped out the energy last night? Did it need to recharge? Was I not focused enough?

"What are you doing?" Came a woman's sharp tone of voice that made me jump.

Julia stood in the center of the hall with her hands on her hips, staring me down. The woman I'd met on my front porch in North Carolina had transformed into the warden of a female prison.

"I thought I…I heard a noise." I stumbled over my words.

"No one's allowed in Aiden's office," she answered hatefully.

"Well, someone's in there. Shouldn't we check?" When Julia didn't move, but appeared to consider this, I added, "Or, we can wait for Aiden. I'm sure he wouldn't be mad we stood out here while someone rifled through his office."

Julia pursed her lips together and waved me out of the way as she produced a key ring from around her wrist. She unlocked the door and pushed it open. Before she could step through, I jumped ahead of her, eager to get inside and survey the room.

The room was large with ornate furnishings and a cathedral-style ceiling, just like all the rooms on the first floor of Carey House. To the left of the door was Aiden's desk which faced the length of the room. Towards the end of the room sat a sofa and two chairs facing a large stone fireplace. The fireplace was almost as wide as the room.

I pointed to a building model sitting on a table between the sofa and chairs, "What's this?" I asked. Was the Order making plans to build a new meeting place somewhere? If that was true, it would be massive, probably as large as the Vatican from the look of the model.

"It's nothing. There's no one here. Let's go!" Julia commanded.

"Are you sure?" I asked, as I walked around a large stone pillar toward the fireplace. Something hung inside the fireplace itself. Julia made a loud, exasperated sound, but I pretended not to hear as I placed my hands on the stone hearth. The top of the hearth sat at least two feet from the floor, and was so wide, I was able to crawl onto it and reach my hand into the fireplace. Drops of black sludge dripped on my hand.

Hanging down, suspended by brass chains, was a darkened brass devil holding a pitchfork. The figure was heavy, covered in soot, and intricately designed, all the way to its hooved feet.

"Leave that alone," Julia barked.

I didn't move. "What is it?"

"It's the damper pull chain for the chimney flue. Now get out of there."

As I backed out of the fireplace, I heard a scratching noise from inside the chimney as Aiden entered his office with Roger in tow. At once, Julia jumped at the opportunity to tell him about me "allegedly" hearing a noise and how we came inside to investigate. Aiden narrowed his eyes and studied my soot covered hands and wrists. The scratching sound stopped at once. No one else acted like they heard it.

"You'd better go and get cleaned up, Ava," he said quietly. He didn't appear angry at all. He seemed…apologetic? Maybe he'd thought about our conversation last night and felt bad about what he'd said to me regarding Jake.

I nodded. "Oh, have you seen Martha this morning?" I asked. It was unusual that the woman wasn't here at Carey House yet. She was here dawn to dusk almost every day.

Aiden set the papers in his hand down on the desk. "No," he answered. "Actually, Martha called me this morning. She's decided to go back to Ireland."

"She decided to go back to Ireland this morning?"

Aiden sat down in his chair and leaned forward. For the first time since I'd met him, he appeared tired. "Yes, she said she misses her family. She's gone." He waved his hand towards the door. "Now, please, Ava. Go and get cleaned up."

As I started towards the door, I heard Roger ask Aiden, "Are you sure you want the pond demolished tomorrow? You just had it built this year at Rachel's request."

"Yes. I said I want it gone," Aiden sounded like he was losing patience with his Number One.

Julia started to follow me out, but Roger shut the door before she could grab her witch's broom and follow me. I stood in the empty hallway and tried to listen through the door, but I couldn't make out what the three of them were saying. Rachel had asked Aiden to build the pond as a subtle way to keep herself charged with an Elemental power source. Was he tearing it down because he knew something about us or because of our exchange last night by the pond? My thoughts floated to Martha. She was scared last night. There was no doubt about that. But for her to make the decision to leave for Ireland this morning after making the comment about the Order never letting her leave? I didn't buy it. Had something happened to the good-natured old woman?

I hurried to the kitchen and removed my bracelet and rings to try to wash the black grime off me. It was more than soot. This felt slimy, oily. As I washed my hands and fingernails, I glanced out the kitchen window, but it was almost impossible to see out the pane of glass.

Dozens of large flies huddled on the inside of the large window. They weren't flying around like normal flies. These congregated together and moved as one back and forth and top to bottom on the left window pane.

Maybe I should go back to Aiden's office and tell Roger or Julia about the sudden infestation. No, I needed a shower. They'd find out on their own. Plus, the thought of dealing with Julia twice in one day was too much.

On the third floor, I paused in front of my room. Goosebumps covered my arms as a cold breeze blew from the stairwell toward me. I suddenly felt drawn to the attic door next to Kory's room. I opened the door a crack and listened. Aiden's Irish brogue drifted down the dark steps.

Had he come to the third floor after he spoke with Roger and Julia? And why was he in the attic of all places?

I opened the door a little farther. A narrow wooden staircase led to the attic floor. I slipped my flip flops off, and leaving the door open, silently stepped onto the bottom step. I expected it to creak, but when it didn't, I continued climbing the stairs.

I heard a man's voice, gruff and commanding, "I told you, boy, the Brewer women are dangerous. You can't see it, but I can in this realm."

"I have it under control, Lyle. I've muted their powers, so they can't interfere with the Order's business," Aiden's voice answered.

Lyle? Was that Lyle Carey, the Founder of the Order of Greatness? The *dead* Lyle Carey?

I stopped on the stairs and laid down, so I could position my head near the top stair to try to get a view of the two men. From this angle, I could see into one of the many smaller rooms in the attic. Aiden stood facing a window, but I couldn't see the other man.

"Muted?" the man retorted. "I saw the older girl blow a dozen trees down last night without trying. No, your feelings for the mother are going to be the downfall of the Order. I met women like them, Elementals, in my lifetime. You might think you're in control of them, but they control you!"

Aiden whirled around on the unseen man. "No one controls me, Ghost. Not Rachel, and certainly, not you. I'm removing their biggest power source here, the pond. If I must, I'll tear down the greenhouse too, with my bare hands. As for the Brewer girls, I can pull Kory into the Order. She's ripe for a higher power." The way he said the word *ripe* made my stomach turn.

The unseen man chuckled. "And what of Ava? Hmmm? I saw the two of you last night. You weren't in control at all. You would have taken her right there on the lawn while her mother slept if she hadn't walked away. She is beginning to channel her Elemental powers and summoning help from the supernatural realm. One such creature was here on the grounds last night. If her actions draw the attention of the Creator-"

"I fear no man, and no thing. This discussion is over, Lyle. I have to prepare for the meeting," Aiden said.

I hurriedly slid down the stairs and through the door, shutting it quietly behind me. I was almost to my room when I realized I'd left my flip flops near the door.

I started after them when the attic door opened. I ducked into the bathroom and locked the door. I stayed in the bathroom for a long while until I was positive Aiden was somewhere else in the house.

I slid out of the bathroom, down the hall, and into my room. I breathed a sigh of relief as I locked the door.

Until I saw my flip flops on the bed.

~ ~ ~

I found Rachel in her bedroom a while later. She was sitting on the bed with her legs crossed in front of her, reading a magazine. A posture I'd seen Kory do a thousand times.

"Can I come in?" I asked from the doorway.

She flipped her magazine closed. "Of course," she smiled.

As I climbed onto the gigantic bed, I couldn't help but notice the magazine was the newest issue of Parents. I suddenly forgot about the real reason I'd gone to look for her. "You're reading Parents? Are you still thinking about having a baby?" I asked.

"Oh, yes!" She answered me way too enthusiastically before her face took on a serious expression. "Look, I know I was a messed-up mom once upon a time when you girls needed me, but I've changed. I'm clean and sober. I'll never allow drugs to rule my life again. I'm going to be a great mom to you and Kory. And the baby." She placed her hand on my arm.

I slid off the bed and went to one of the open balcony doors. "Does Aiden want a baby right now too?" I asked.

"Well," she answered slowly, "he wants a baby in time. His responsibilities here are great and I think he wants to make sure I can handle motherhood first. That I don't get overwhelmed."

"So, Kory and I are the guinea pigs," I said as I watched two figures walking along the path in the backyard.

Rachel moved off the bed and walked out onto the balcony. She turned to face me as she leaned against the railing. "Not guinea pigs, Ava. You're my daughters and I love you very much. It's hard for me to remember that I have to be your parent and not just your friend."

I bit my tongue from pointing out the fact that she wasn't my friend as I watched the two people below approach Carey House. I walked to the balcony railing when I realized it was Kory and Aiden. Kory looked up and waved. What was she doing out there with Aiden? I thought about his words to me last night by the pond and his conversation with Lyle Carey's ghost.

"What do you know about Aiden? About where he's from, his family? You don't know if he would make a good father," I whispered to Rachel. Kory and Aiden disappeared from my view. Probably headed for the back door.

Rachel moved closer to me, the smile gone. "I know him. He's a good man raised by his grandmother after the death of his parents in a train derailment. He went to Dublin City University and graduated with Honors before moving to the States. He's generous and kind and helps people – just ask your new friend, Jake. He's doing a good thing here and it has potential to expand across the nation. Without him, I would probably still be homeless and drugged-up somewhere. I wouldn't be the person I am today." She took a deep breath and sighed as she observed the landscape. She reminded me of a queen surveying her estate. She only needed her crown.

Before I could say anything else to her in regard to Aiden, the man himself walked into the bedroom.

"Ah good, Ava, you're still here. I wanted to see if we could talk for a few minutes." He leaned against the balcony doorway and crossed his arms.

"What about?" I asked as I remembered last night's awkward moment and what Lyle Carey had said could have happened. Rachel patted my shoulder.

"You two do need to talk. I'll be in the den," she gave Aiden a quick kiss on the lips, grabbed her magazine off the bed, and left the room.

Aiden motioned for me to sit on one of the chairs on the balcony as he took the other and scooted it closer. He leaned forward with his elbows on his knees, his hands together. He still looked tired.

"I want to apologize for last night. I accused you of meeting Jake, and then I preceded to try to talk to you about things that are apparently your mother's forte." When I didn't answer, he continued. "When I was a boy growing up in Ireland, I lived with my grandmother after my parents died. Although I worked hard in school and around town, as a teenager I got myself involved with a local girl. It didn't work out and I was heartbroken, but I'm glad now that our relationship ended. If not, I probably wouldn't have gone on to University or relocated here. I would've never met your mother," he paused. "I just don't want to see you get hurt by a boy. We're stupid sometimes," he chuckled at his own joke.

I nodded my head as I mustered a smile. Since he was having this heart-to-heart now, should I ask him about Lyle Carey's ghost? Somehow, this didn't seem like the right time to accuse Aiden of harboring ghosts and demons within the confines of Carey House or demand that he leave the pond in place as our Elemental energy resource. He reached over and placed his hand on mine on the arm of the chair.

"Listen, I know you suspect me of stealing away your mother while playing the evil stepfather, but that couldn't be further from the truth. I love Rachel very much and I want nothing more than to have you and your sister here. Yes, I do get angry when I think you are defying me, but this is my first time as a parent to two teenage girls." He threw up both hands in a gesture of surrender which was oddly funny for Aiden. I laughed a little and this seemed to please him.

"As you can see, Kory is adjusting perfectly here and now she's excited about school starting next month. She's very sociable and I don't think she'll have any problem making new friends. I wanted to let you know, that if you want to return to the house in Locklyn, I won't stop you. You can attend your senior year of school there and we can all get together for the holidays and your graduation."

I blinked. I could go home? He was right about Kory. And I could always have Jake keep an eye out for her, at least until he left for college. If we found the demon soon, then Rachel and Kory wouldn't need me to stay. It was clear that my sister loved me, but she was ready to have a mother-daughter relationship with Rachel.

"You'd have to promise me that the Order would not use Iris' house for any reason. It would just be me. No caretakers, no cleaning ladies, no members. I would live there as before."

Aiden leaned back in his chair. A businessman like him knew the value of a bargaining chip. He ran his hand over his chin, and then leaned forward again. "The Order will have business in Locklyn, but no Order at your home at all. Strictly yours. We, as in your mother, Kory, and myself, would only stay there while visiting you."

"No Order business in Locklyn either. It's my hometown. The Order could expand into the other tourist towns like Holden Beach, Supply, or Shallotte."

I could see the wheels turning in his head.

"Only one meeting site in Locklyn in a rural area outside the city limits and nowhere else. Especially near your home," he countered while his gaze remained steady.

I nodded my head. "Give me time to think about it. It will be hard to leave Kory."

"Of course, I understand. I won't take up any more of your time and I have to go over a few things before the meeting," he said as he sat back in his chair.

Before I left him, I stopped at the bedroom door as a thought crossed my mind.

"Aiden, what happened to her?"

He turned around in the chair to look at me. "Who?"

"The girl who broke your heart in Ireland."

Even from the bedroom door, I could see Aiden's jaw clench. I'd hit a nerve. Almost immediately, he relaxed his face into a smile. "Nothing, I suppose. I heard she had a baby," he shrugged as he turned back around in his chair to face the landscape.

I quietly left him and went to my bedroom.

~ ~ ~

I didn't see Rachel or Kory the rest of the day until evening, mostly because I stayed in my room to avoid Aiden, Julia, and the other members. The conversation with Aiden on the balcony and his proposition replayed in my mind, but I already knew my answer. Even if Kory was ready for this 'traditional' family, she didn't know about Lyle Carey or what secrets had scared Martha. I wanted to ask more about the girl in Ireland with the baby. Had it been Aiden's baby? Was that why they broke up? Was that the real reason why he wanted to wait to have a baby with Rachel? The baby would be in his or her late teens by now, I would guess. More than likely, his sharing his past about the girl with the baby was completely unrelated to what was happening at Carey House and was only meant to deter me from having a serious relationship with Jake. But I still wondered if Rachel knew.

I did venture out of the safety of my room to "borrow" a slinky top from Kory's closet to wear with my skinny jeans and ballet flats while getting dressed to meet Jake at six.

As I dressed, I thought about the conversation between Aiden and the spirit of Lyle Carey. The ghost had seen Calder and was clearly aware of who and what we were. Even worse, Aiden knew. Rachel believed she kept Aiden in the dark regarding the Siren myth and our matriarchal Elemental powers, but it was Aiden playing the clueless fiancé. To what end? What exactly was the Order of Greatness hiding?

I couldn't tell Rachel, not yet. Not until I discovered what was happening at Carey House. If a powerful demon controlled the Order, the one who once inhabited Lyle Carey, where had it gone? Aiden was charismatic and controlling, but he wasn't the picture of a possessed man. At least, not like the ones in the movies.

Now was the time to find out the secrets the Order kept and maybe Jake would give them up tonight. That is if he knew anything. How much would Aiden divulge to a nineteen-year-old boy? Then again, it seemed Aiden had plans to groom Jake. Was it to possibly lead the Order one day?

Playing it cool, I made my way down the stairs. People were beginning to congregate in the Great Hall to socialize, but I didn't see Jake in the crowd. I walked to the dining room, smiling at random members as I passed, until I reached the back door. Slipping out, I looked around to make sure no members-slash-landscapers were hanging around, and then made a quick run to the greenhouse. Jake hadn't made it yet, so I went to the far end of the greenhouse and hunkered down on the floor to wait. The smell of dirt and blooming flowers was strong, yet there was another scent I couldn't identify – almost metallic.

Fifteen minutes passed before I heard the door open. I held my breath, hoping it was indeed Jake, and not another member.

"Ava," Jake whispered loudly, "you here?"

"Hey," I sat up on my knees and waved him over.

"Why are you sitting in the dark? And what is that weird smell?" But, even as he asked the question, he sat down on the floor in front of me and crossed his legs. He'd brought two cups of coffee with him and handed me one. Although it was warm outside, the heat from the tall mug was comforting.

"This reminds me, did you see those flies in the kitchen window?" I asked.

"What flies?"

"There were dozens of them on the window this morning. Giant horseflies."

"No, there aren't any flies in the kitchen. Is that what you wanted to ask me? About flies?" He winked.

I shook my head. Roger must've sprayed them earlier in the day. "No, never mind about the flies. I don't want anyone from the Order to know we're in here. Look, Jake, the truth is I don't know about these people. I mean the members, and the entire Order for that matter. They're a religious organization of what? All religions worship something, but what does the Order worship? Self? Aiden?" I took a sip of my coffee as Jake seemed to consider my words.

Finally, he shrugged. "When my parents died it was Aiden and the Order that got me through it. Livin' with my uncle hasn't been easy, but the members have been there for me. I've learned I can do so much, be so much more. Believin' in them and helping out is a small price to pay for the support." He stopped talking, but I could see a flicker of discontent behind his eyes.

I finished the thought for him, "But, you're thinking there has to be more. There has to be a God."

Jake frowned and sat up straighter. "Why? Why would there have to be a God?" Apparently, I'd hit a nerve.

"Because you know deep down, we didn't create this universe. Someone else did. A Creator designed it all, including a spiritual realm, a plane, we can't see, with everything mapped out. Everything around us buzzes with an energy down to the very molecules. We make our choices and He really wants us to turn to Him and ask for help. Self and secrets are the basis for the Order's belief system and I can't shake this feeling that God, Creator, Higher Power, whatever you want to call It, is losing patience with their otherworldly influence. It's not a matter of a man with a sinister modus operandi. Something's wrong here."

Jake's eyes studied my face in the moonlight. Was I getting through to him at all? He ran his hand through his short blond hair and took a deep breath.

"That's the stupidest thing I've ever heard. And I've heard a lot." He grinned and took a swig of his coffee. "Okay, I grant you that sometimes the members do ask me to do things I think maybe I shouldn't. But, you gotta realize these people are like family to me. Aiden made sure certain doors opened for me. Before, the thought of college was like a dream for a poor kid like me from the holler. Maybe if I'd worked hard in school I could have done it on my own, but I didn't. Aiden made one phone call and a private university accepted me to start in the Fall. How can I question that?"

I leaned against the wall and pulled my knees to my chest, hugging the coffee mug. Aiden had made one phone call and changed the trajectory of Jake's life. He had made one phone call and changed the meeting for the reading of the will, thus changing the trajectory of my life. How could one man have such an influential power? How could he pull so many strings at once? Was it savvy social networking or did he have something on those people in charge? I closed my eyes trying to clear my head. It seemed the more I found out about the Order, the more intricate things became, and now Jake probably thought I was insane. He didn't know about Elementals and energy and supernatural beings with powers.

I felt Jake's hand on my knee. "My turn. You said you don't trust the Order, why?"

I told him about Aiden and Rachel's arrival at Iris' funeral, and how our lives turned upside down and inside out within a matter of days. I told him how Aiden's influence seemed to have no boundaries. I also told him about Julia trying to stop me from going into Aiden's office today.

"I think the members are watching me. If I push a boundary, like Aiden's office, they run to him tattling the whole way." I thought about the ghost of Lyle Carey, but I might wind up in an asylum if I told Jake.

"Not to sound mean, but I think you may be a bit paranoid. As far as I can tell, the members seem to like havin' you and Kory here. Have you told your mother about any of this?" Jake asked, pulling a piece of gum from his pocket and popping it into his mouth.

"No, not yet. When she first came back into our lives, I had a hard time forgiving her for abandoning us eight years ago. But, after spending time with her I can see that her life was really messed up, and if we had stayed with her, our childhood may have been just as messed up. Our aunt Iris was wonderful." My eyes grew hot and I took a deep breath to get control. I didn't want to cry in front of Jake.

He scooted a little closer to me. "Ava, I could see that about you and your sister. I'll admit, I was a little intimidated by you when we first met because it seemed like you guys had it all and never had to struggle. Now I see your struggle was just on the inside."

He was right. On the outside Kory and I wanted for nothing and thanks to Iris, we never had. Inside was a different story, especially when it came to Rachel and the father I never knew. "Rachel is trying hard to be the mother she should've been all along. Kory is willing to jump right in with her, but I can't. I mean I know she's changed. And I know she loves Aiden, and I think he makes her happy. If I tell her my suspicions, it will drive a deeper wedge between us."

I pulled my legs closer as a gust of air came through the greenhouse. Jake looked around.

"That's weird. The greenhouse is usually humid. It feels downright cold in here now. I think it's warmer outside." He set down his mug and crossed his arms over his chest, shielding him from the cold air.

"I was thinking the same thing."

My insides began to tremble, and I wasn't sure if it was the sudden chill or the beginning of a vision.

Not now. Not with Jake here.

A shuffling sound came from the far corner of the room. Jake and I both rose to our feet; keenly aware we were no longer alone. I could barely make out the outline of a man in a dress shirt, his back to me. Had another member heard our discussion? Would they run to Aiden?

As the man slowly turned, I realized who had invaded the greenhouse. Not who, but what. The ghost of the possessed Lyle Carey. I stepped forward, preparing to face the creature down. Jake picked up the pruning shears. If he could see it, then it was solid now. Stronger.

Before I could question Jake on what exactly he could see, Lyle's ghost started at us. Jake raised the shears and hollered for him to get out. Without hesitation, I extended my arms. Nothing happened. No beams of light. No energy balls.

The spirit ran toward us, and before we could dodge it, it moved through us. A wave of nausea hit me as it passed through, a cold presence in my bones. We both turned in time to see it disappear into the greenhouse wall.

The room was dark and quiet again.

Jake put the shears down on the table. "What was that?" His voice sounded strained as if he wasn't quite sure what he had seen. At this point, I wasn't quite sure what he had seen either.

Where was my Elemental power? For Pete's sake, I was standing in a greenhouse with plenty of earth and soil surrounding me to use as a resource. All that training with Calder, but when it came down to defending Jake and myself, I'd choked. I couldn't defeat a powerful demon if I couldn't even fend off the ghost of an old man.

"Ava?" Jake's voice interrupted my thoughts. "Are you alright?"

I nodded my head as I stared at my normal-looking hands. "That was the real live ghost of Lyle Carey, the Founder of the Order of Greatness." I announced, wishing I'd chosen a better description.

Jake walked over and touched the wall where Lyle's ghost had disappeared through moments ago. "It was real," he said. "I saw him. I don't think anyone will believe us though." He looked at me over his shoulder.

"No, they won't. Up until now, you didn't believe me about spiritual realms or otherworldly planes of existence either."

Jake, deep in thought, walked over to me, and ran his hands up and down my arms. I hadn't realized goosebumps covered my exposed skin. I could smell the gum he must've swallowed.

"What else are you right about?" He asked.

Somehow, I didn't think he really wanted to hear the answer.

CHAPTER TWENTY-FIVE

Jake walked back to Carey House with me and as we entered the crowded dining room, we were met with stares from the talkative members. As we reached the Great Hall, someone called his name and Jake disappeared into the crowd. I found my way over to the staircase and leaned against the railing. Several members looked over at me and spoke to each other, but no one spoke to me.

"Hey, there you are," Kory said from behind me. "I went to your room to get you, but you had already taken off. Nice top, by the way," she said, as she eyeballed her fantastic-looking shirt on me.

"Yeah, I wanted to see how many people come to these things. What do you think they'll talk about?"

Kory shrugged and stood on the bottom stair. She leaned over the railing to put her face close to mine. "I don't know but try to have an open mind. I know you are dying to catch Aiden and these people up to something, but it is probably just like a regular church gathering." She absent-mindedly played with the charms on her wrist.

I narrowed my eyes at my sister. I'd allowed her to spend too much time with Rachel and Aiden and this was the result. Nothing had been "regular" since Iris died. "What were you and Aiden talking about this morning?"

She shrugged. "I'd gone for a walk and ran into him coming out of the greenhouse. We had a good talk."

"A good talk about what?"

"Just life stuff, okay?" I narrowed my eyes again at her, so she continued as she shook her head. "He said that this place was good for me and he couldn't wait for me to make new friends. Not just in the Order, but in the community. He said when he first met me, he thought I was a bit self-absorbed, but now he's seen me act more mature than my fifteen years," she snapped her charm bracelet on her wrist. "So, you can stop being all judgy about him and these people," she added.

I rolled my eyes, but before I could tell her where to stick her charms, Rachel came over to us.

"Come on, girls. We should go ahead and get seated. Everyone will follow us."

I touched Rachel's arm. "Can we talk for a second? Privately?" I asked. Rachel glanced at the crowd and then motioned for me to follow her. Kory just shrugged and resumed her perch on the staircase.

Rachel led me to a door under the stairs and I followed her onto the dimly lit staircase. I was glad when she stopped on the landing as the steps below us seemed to stretch into an abyss.

"Now, what is it? We have to get back up there before Aiden starts the meeting. There are new people here – visitors – which means potential new members." Rachel was clearly not pleased with my request for her time.

"Something resembling the late possessed Lyle Carey tried to attack me in the greenhouse."

Rachel stopped fidgeting with her bracelet. "Lyle Carey? When?" She asked.

"Not twenty minutes ago."

She clucked her tongue. "Ava, Calder taught you how to vanquish apparitions. Did you do it?"

"I tried, but my powers didn't work. The ghost passed right through me, but did you hear me? It was Lyle Carey."

Rachel tugged on my arm, leading me back up the steps. "Well, come on. We can talk about this later."

"Wait!" I said, a bit too loudly as we reached the top of the stairs and Rachel hushed me. With her hand on the doorknob, she exhaled loudly, apparently tired of my supernatural teen drama. I continued anyway, "I think Aiden knows about us."

"What?" The color drained from her face.

"I overheard..." I trailed off not sure what to tell her exactly. Should I reveal to her about sneaking into the attic, breaking into the Meeting room, conning Julia into opening Aiden's office door, kissing Calder by the pond, or luring Aiden unintentionally?

"Overheard what, Ava?" Now it was her turn to raise her voice.

"What if it's him?" I blurted out, not at all what I wanted to lead with. "What if Aiden's the possessed man? What if it's a demon controlling the Order? We've been busy looking around town for it, but it might be here." I took a deep breath. "Maybe in your bed," I added.

"That's enough. What are you talking about? I would know if it were Aiden." She struggled to keep her voice low.

"Would you? You're so caught up with trying to please him to stay in his good graces that you're already blind to the Order's influence and scare tactics. I think he used your Elemental energy in Locklyn to set up a meeting with Freya's dad." A surprised look crossed Rachel's face. I pushed on. "Did you know there are members here who are afraid to question Aiden? I overheard Aiden and – " the narrow door jerked open and Rachel and I both yelped. Roger stood in the doorway.

"Sorry, Rachel, but Aiden is looking for you." Roger's deep voice filled the small corridor. We followed him out from under the stairs and Kory joined us as we moved silently to the Meeting room. Rachel and I would need to finish our conversation, but was there any use? It seemed she would defend Aiden until her dying day. What would she say when I told her about Aiden and Lyle's ghost? Would she shrug that off too?

As we entered the Meeting room, I noticed the large mirror that hung on the left side of the door was cracked, shattered at the bottom. Had someone punched the glass? I suddenly remembered the morning Aiden had cut his hand. Had he punched the mirror? It was missing a large piece from the bottom right-hand corner. A shard probably three inches long.

Certainly, the missing mirror shard couldn't be the same one I found in the garden in Locklyn. How would it have gotten there and why? My head began to spin as I searched for our seats.

As we sat down on the front row, I turned in my seat to get a better view of the room from this vantage point instead of the stage. The vaulted ceiling resembled the ceilings in the Great Hall and Aiden's office. Tall stained-glass windows ran along the far wall. These were the windows I could see from the greenhouse, but unfortunately could not see in or out of them. The walls were stone like something from a medieval castle and cloth banners hung in various places with the strange symbols sewn onto them. I caught a glimpse of Jake who smiled at me before turning his attention back to a member.

Aiden walked by on his way to the stage and gave Rachel a quick kiss. To my surprise, he winked at my sister who smiled so wide I could see her molars. He didn't look in my direction at all. The Aiden I talked with on his balcony was gone. This Aiden didn't look tired, but invigorated. Perhaps he'd already figured out that I wouldn't take him up on his offer to move back to North Carolina. Lyle Carey's ghost had insisted that Aiden wasn't in control last night on the lawn. He'd said that I'd controlled Aiden. Maybe Aiden wanted little to do with me if he thought that was true. Truth be told, it probably was true. My make-out session with Calder had caused me to unintentionally lure Aiden. I needed to stop thinking about what could've happened if I hadn't walked away, as Lyle's ghost had insinuated.

Kory nudged me. "What do those symbols mean?" She nodded her head toward the banners on the walls that held the same symbols from the scroll.

"I don't know. I was wondering the same thing but didn't want to open my mouth to ask you."

Kory made a face at me and reached past me to Rachel, tapping her on the arm.

"Mom, what are those symbols?"

Rachel whispered back, "I'll tell you later."

"What is that thing?" I asked, pointing to a large pillar near the stage. It was like the one in Aiden's office, but stood at least seven feet tall with a pointed top. It was covered in the symbols, all along its corners. It reminded me of the Washington Monument when I visited Washington, D.C. on my Fifth-grade trip. Except the Washington Monument wasn't ancient and housed in a medieval sanctuary of sorts. How had I missed this when I broke into the Meeting room? Had it always been here?

Rachel whispered back, "It's an Ogham stone. One of the oldest in existence. Aiden had it brought here from Ireland. I'll tell you more later." She pointed upfront and put her finger to her lips as a silent hush filled the room.

Rachel knew what the symbols meant. I made a mental note to ask her later and not tell her about me breaking into the Meeting Room and stealing the scroll. She was aggravated enough with me today.

A sweater and trouser clad Aiden stepped onto the stage. I am not sure what I expected, maybe him wearing a robe? Once behind the podium, he looked out at the members and smiled his overly used charming smile. I glanced at Kory and Rachel. Kory leaned back in the pew. Maybe she was contemplating the symbols. Rachel sat back as well, full attention on Aiden, wearing an encouraging smile across her face.

Aiden started his speech.

The next few moments became a blur as everything happened so fast. The phone in my back pocket vibrated. As inconspicuously as possible, I shifted in my seat until I pulled the iPhone out of my skinny jeans that were not made to hold cell phones while the wearer sat on a wooden pew. The text was from Jake. It read only four words.

You may be right.

Before I could answer his text, Aiden cleared his throat and I realized he was looking at me as he spoke. Apparently texting on a cell phone is rude in a cult as well as in other meeting places. I slid my phone back into my pocket as I felt Kory silently laugh.

Rachel, however, gave me the stink eye over it.

Instead of listening, I concentrated on memorizing the symbols from the banners. Maybe Calder knew something about them by now. Each symbol resembled sticks with lines crossing through them. Some went left to right, while others were vertical. The ones carved into the Ogham stone appeared crude, as if done by a semi-sharp instrument. Or perhaps the stone had once been outside and weathered by the elements.

As I continued to focus on the symbols, my insides began to tremble. Not now. Not in front of all these people. Would I see the ghost of Lyle Carey again or an actual demon this time? If Jake saw the last apparition, would the entire Order share in my vision now?

I closed my eyes and hoped no one noticed my tremors. With my eyes closed, I managed to tune Aiden's lecture out and remain calm, breathing slow deep breaths while enjoying the silence in my head.

Until I heard Calder's voice.

Ava, I'm going to set you free. Open your eyes.

I opened my eyes in time to see my arms raised out in front of me, hands clenched into fists. Before I could lower my arms, the charm bracelet I wore flew apart and hovered for a second before the charms shot towards the stage area. Aiden turned his head to keep from getting hit with the shower of charms and beads.

The people gasped.

"It's alright, everyone," he smiled at his congregation. "It appears my stepdaughter Ava has had a wardrobe malfunction. Let's get back to the meeting." He laughed softly as if amused by my antic.

I hurried out of the Meeting room thoroughly embarrassed. When I got to the Great Hall I stopped in front of the fireplace. I heard Kory quickly approaching.

"Ava, what was that?" She stage whispered to me. It didn't matter. The Meeting room was out of hearing distance.

I put my hands up to my head and dug my fingers into my hair, into my scalp, until I could feel pain. Before I could answer her, my phone vibrated. I whipped it out of my pocket. It was Jake asking the same question. I shoved the phone back in my pocket without answering him either.

I sat down heavily on the floor in front of the fireplace. Kory's eyes looked wild from worry. "What did you see me do?" I asked her.

"You raised your arms and pointed at Aiden, and then made a fist at him. You launched your bracelet at him." She waved her arms dramatically, and I hoped I didn't look half as manic.

I laid on the cold marble floor, closed my eyes, and laughed. As Kory kneeled beside me, I opened my eyes.

"The bracelet came apart and all the pieces flew at him. I didn't do it. I think Cadler did."

"Calder?" Kory stage whispered again. She stood up as rage crossed her dark eyes. "Was it really Calder or is that your excuse this time? I know we've learned a lot about who we are since Iris died, but I think you can't stand being here. Even knowing you are an Elemental with powers, you can't stand having real parents or rules. You know you need to forgive Mom because you want her in your life, but you can't admit it. I think you want the demon to be Aiden because that would be easier for you. Why can't you accept that Mom loves him, and he is going to be our stepfather and this-," she waved her arms around again – "is going to be our home?!"

I stared at the ceiling and wondered where to begin. The Order and Aiden had brainwashed Kory already. She didn't believe anything I told her. As for my forgiving Rachel...

I shut my eyes again. I would have a bigger storm to face when the meeting ended.

CHAPTER TWENTY-SIX

Unfortunately, I was right.

Before the end of the meeting, I made sure I was out of sight, and hopefully, out of Aiden's mind. Kory decided to rejoin the meeting and work interference on my behalf. Maybe she could somehow explain to Rachel and Aiden that I didn't really mean to throw my belongings across the room. If Kory could convince Rachel that it was Calder, maybe she would believe.

Calder. He'd said he was setting me free. What did that mean?

It was a long while before I heard the heated voice of Rachel coming up the stairs. Strangely, I couldn't hear Aiden's response. I'd been lying across the bed, so I sat up waiting for Aiden to pound on the door.

Instead, the bedroom door burst open as if a powerful hurricane wind had pushed the door. Aiden stood in the doorway, hatred and rage crossing his face. I leapt from the bed, but he caught me by the throat and slammed me hard against the bedroom wall. Rachel screamed.

He held me against the wall by only one outstretched arm as I scratched at his hand. He squeezed tighter. I felt a popping sensation in my throat as I tasted blood. If I could only focus long enough to summon the Elemental energy…

Through bleary eyes, I saw Rachel grabbing at Aiden's arm and pulling him, but he didn't move. Instead, he pulled me closer to his face, and then slammed the back of my head again into to the wall. Again, Rachel screamed.

He turned his head, and growled at her, "Leave. Now. Stay in your room."

Rachel started to protest, and then moved silently to the doorway. I clutched at Aiden's hand and tried to kick him with my legs, but somehow, he'd pinned me to the wall. I rolled my eyes toward the hall in time to see my mother disappear.

He's killing me.

The charmer was gone. This was the real Aiden. And Rachel had left me to face him alone.

"Stop fighting me." He pulled me away from the wall only to slam my head back into it. I struggled to stay awake, struggled to breathe.

"Tell me something, Ava. How did you know about the bracelet? That it strips you Brewer women of your power and stops you from accessing the elements?"

With his free hand, he pulled something out of his pocket and held it to my face. It was half of my owl charm from the bracelet.

When I didn't answer him, he put his mouth close to my ear and hissed, "You left this behind when you broke into the Meeting room. I control the other two Elementals. Around me, they have no power, they do as I command, but not you. Why is that?"

He pulled his face away from mine as he tightened his grip around my throat. "The bracelet worked on you for a while. It's almost laughable how you thought you were using your ability on me in Locklyn. Trust me, I thought about letting you continue – see how far you'd go to get your way." His eyes, no longer dark, appeared lifeless and covered with a film, a silver glaze.

The eyes of a dead man.

"I could kill you right now, but I'm not. Things could have been different. You could've sat at my right hand." His voice sounded almost normal again. "You're not going to take Rachel and Kory down with you, or any of the members of the Order, including Jake. Oh, that's right, I know about you and Jake. I know all about the doubts you planted in his head – my protégé. I've worked hard to prepare him to lead the Order one day and you fill his mind with doubts. You're going to run away tonight, never heard from again. If you ever step foot near Carey House again, I'll kill you. If you ever come around Rachel or Kory, I'll kill your sister in front of you."

He let go and I dropped to the floor in a heap. My throat burned as I gasped for air. I couldn't breathe, let alone summon any Elemental energy. Where was Kory?

Aiden towered over me. He wore his charming smile in contrast to his sadistic eyes as he kicked me hard in the stomach.

The air escaped me and I struggled to fill my burning lungs again. My throat stung as I whispered through tears, "I will never let you hurt them."

His grin widened as he shook his head, and then he punched me in the face. After that, everything went dark.

CHAPTER TWENTY-SEVEN

Cold.

I tried to open my eyes, but the pain in my head forced me to squeeze them shut again. I laid still, not knowing where I was, trying to remember all of the events from the evening.

Then I remembered.

Aiden almost killed me. His last words to me had been a warning - I had better disappear or he would kill me. That was right before he punched me in the face. At that thought, my head began to pound. I spread my hands and allowed my fingers to explore the surface under me. Grass and dirt.

The chirping of crickets only served as antagonists to my aching head as I slowly opened my eyes. It was still dark. I focused on the little bright lights above and realized they were stars. It'd been a long time since I'd laid on the ground, looking up at the stars. Last time had been in the back yard at home in Locklyn when I was ten with Iris pointing out the constellations.

I raised my hand to wipe a tear from my face. The right side along the cheekbone felt swollen.

The demon possessed Aiden.

I shut my eyes again as the tears made the night sky blurry. Aiden was the reason for the visions. He was why our Elemental powers surfaced at this time in our lives, why Rachel was so attracted to him. He was the demon. The demon my mother left in a room with me.

I forced my groaning body to turn over and buried my face in the cool grass. I laid there a long time sobbing, not only hurt physically from Aiden, but emotionally from Rachel's betrayal, and the fear of what might happen to Kory now.

I breathed in the muskiness of the ground beneath me and managed to pull my legs under my chest, stretching my arms in front of me into child's pose. My right arm shook with the immense pain piercing my lung as the muscles along my hips, back, and shoulders screamed in unison. Digging my fingers deeper into the dirt, I focused on the energy emanating from the ground. I imagined the energy as a ball of light, like Calder taught me, and concentrated on moving the light from my hands, through my arms, and over my back. I would have thought that laying in the dirt would produce more energy, but the light came in spurts. The energy burned, but I didn't let it go. I couldn't. I needed every bit of it to help me move.

I screamed in agony as the energy tugged and twisted at a rib. Was it broken? But, as the energy moved over my body in waves, the pain began to subside.

Eventually, I pushed myself back onto my legs and rested my hands on my knees. My head swam as my vision cleared. I was in a field near the woods. Two lonely picnic tables sat in the distance next to a parking lot under a single street lamp. Farther away, I could make out picnic shelters and a building. Was it a restroom building? Was this the designated picnic area in a forest?

Wherever I was, someone was bound to come. I stood up, almost dropping to my knees again as I stumbled. I still wore my jeans and top, but no purse or cell phone. As I willed my legs to move, I noticed the dirt caked on the tops of my flats. I could only imagine which members of The Order had unquestioningly dragged my unconscious body to this place.

I needed help.

I finally made my way to a table and collapsed on top of it, the restroom building just too far away. Maybe after I rested, I would try again. As I stared at the night sky, I didn't care if the table was home to tiny spiders or ants.

For the first time in my life, I was truly alone.

~ ~ ~

"Ava. Ava, wake up."

I shifted and opened my eyes. Iris sat beside me on the picnic table in broad daylight. As I struggled to sit up, she reached her hand under my back and helped lift me upright. As I stared into her eyes, I realized she looked different. Younger, much younger. Perhaps the way Iris had looked in the prime of her life, maybe her thirties, with her blonde hair cut short and swept off to the side. Not one wrinkle adorned her face. I couldn't believe how much Iris and Rachel resembled one another.

"This isn't real, is it?" I asked, my face scrunching up into an ugly cry waiting to happen. She held up the blue stone between her index finger and thumb.

"It's like a vision. As for being real, I guess that depends on which side of the realm you're sitting on." She pushed my hair away from my face, and without warning, I grabbed her around the waist and into a hug. It didn't matter to me if Iris disappeared right then, I needed to feel her.

But she didn't disappear. Instead she wrapped her arms around me and rocked back and forth as I cried. She smelled of flowers and her arms were no longer frail but strong. As she rocked, she hummed softly the way she used to when I was a little girl. I raised my head up to ask her questions, but I didn't know where to start. Instead, Iris nestled her face into my hair as I sobbed.

Finally, she leaned back and cupped my chin in her hands, forcing me to look into those beautiful blue eyes once more. "You feel as if you are alone, but you're not. You've never been. All of heaven is rooting for you. This demon is strong, but already defeated. He's afraid of you because he can't control you. Everything you need, you already possess, Ava."

"I don't know what that means," I caught my breath between sobs. "Iris, I'm scared. Really scared."

Iris' smile never wavered. "I know you are and I know it's hard. But to stop evil, you must do the hard things and lean into that fear. Fear is like a wall. If you lean into it hard enough, the wall will crumble, and your strength will emerge. You have no reason to fear because you've already won, but you must stop giving the enemy ammunition. You need to extend grace and forgive your mother for her past."

I laid my head back onto Iris' lap as if I was still that little girl. "I miss you so much," I whispered through my hot tears.

"I love you, Ava." She sat up straighter on the table. "Now, it's time you wake up. You have work to do."

~ ~ ~

I awakened to bright lights and an excruciating noise. Ignoring the pain in my head, I tried to get my bearings by moving my fingers slowly until they found cool metal. The railing of a hospital bed.

I startled when the automatic blood pressure cuff activated on my right arm. The motion caused me to brush against the IV attached to my left wrist; the stinging reminding me why I hated hospitals. As the monitor beeped, I moved the sheet off me only to discover my clothes were gone. The staff had washed the dirt off and I wore a fresh hospital gown. Although the embarrassment of being dressed by strangers was hard to ignore, I managed to push those thoughts to the side.

I had more important things to worry about than who had seen me naked.

A curtain separated the bed from the remainder of the room, so I listened intently for a roommate or hospital staff, but the room was quiet except for the sound of the blood pressure monitor as it reported my results. I pulled the too-tight cuff off my arm and scooted to the edge of the bed. One glance out the window on the right side of the curtain told me I was on the third floor. If I was going to leave this hospital I would have to use the door.

Peering through the curtain, I confirmed that I didn't share my room with another person which made it easy to search the cabinets for my clothing. The third cabinet held a yellow plastic bag with my dirty clothes inside. I tiptoed to the small bathroom, pulling the IV stand with me, ignoring the mirror hanging above the sink. I would look at my face and the damage done after I dressed.

I braced myself against the wall and pulled the butterfly IV needle out of the side of my wrist. Fighting the urge to pass out, I placed the IV bag in the sink, and then quickly pulled my clothes on. My arms and legs shook as I lifted them. The smell of dirt and blood invaded my nostrils, but this certainly wasn't the time to wash clothes. I needed to get out of this place and figure out what to do.

If I could do anything.

I found several band aids in a drawer by the bed and stuck two over the bleeding spot on my wrist. As I turned to toss the paper into the trash, I caught a glimpse of myself in the mirror and froze. The girl looking back at me wasn't the same girl who had met Jake at the greenhouse. My clothes were dingy and my hair wild. Although I was clean I appeared unkempt. Like I belonged in the hospital. My face was swollen, and the right side sported black and purple patches from the bottom of my eye to the jawline.

My power had healed parts of me, most likely a broken rib. But it hadn't been enough. Knowing my time was short, I placed my hands on my face and closed my eyes. This wasn't like with the cancer that had riddled Iris' body. This was just a surface healing. Something small.

I focused on the image of my face in my mind's eye. The way my complexion was normally creamy and clear. I could see my face from before the confrontation with Aiden as a sigh escaped my mouth from the comforting heat transferring from my hands to my face.

Someone opened the door.

"Whoa," said a young nurse who looked to be but a few years older than me and somewhat familiar. "You're awake. You need to get back into bed."

I held up my hand. "Stop," I said a little too loudly since I hadn't spoken since the night Aiden almost choked the life out of me.

The young nurse narrowed her eyes into slits. "This is exactly what Aiden said would happen. What's wrong, honey? Is it withdrawal?"

"What?" I asked.

She'd said Aiden. Now I knew why she was familiar. She was the girl I'd seen at the greenhouse before the meeting. Aiden's so-called favorite, according to Jake.

D'Netta.

D'Netta continued, "It's okay. Really. We understand here. Aiden told us about your drug problem."

"I don't have a drug problem," I said, getting angry. What had Aiden told these people? Clearly D'Netta was involved.

"Honey, you tested positive for methamphetamines. We are going to help you get better. It'll be okay." She moved towards me and I felt a bit of warmth leave my hands.

Be careful, Ava. This girl is not a tree.

"Stop," I said with my arms outstretched. "I don't want to hurt you."

The nurse stopped as if considering my veiled threat. Suddenly, she lunged forward reaching for my wrist.

The power left my hands and knocked her backwards onto the floor. She hit the back of her head with a thud, but I didn't have time to check on her other than to watch the rising and fall of her chest. Instead I made my way down the hall trying to look nonchalant as I hurried past the nurses' station. I finally spotted a stairwell and prayed the door wouldn't set off an alarm. I bolted down the three flights of stairs until I found an outside door.

In the blinding daylight, I had no idea of the time or where I was. All I knew was I needed to get some place safe and figure out how far Aiden's influence stretched.

CHAPTER TWENTY-EIGHT

I stuck to the trees and alleys, mostly lost in my thoughts, not really knowing where a safe place could be found. I knew if I could get to the coast I could probably summon Calder for help. Rachel had said Iris never needed to summon Calder, but I couldn't seem to focus long enough to think about him.

But at this point, I didn't even know how to get to the coast or even where I was. I walked a long time when I got tired of running. I kept thinking about what D'Netta said about finding methamphetamines in my system. I'd never done drugs and never would. I would never be like Rachel. Was the nurse lying? Somehow, I didn't think so. If there was junk in my system, then that would explain why I couldn't focus my power and summon Calder by thought.

I could have killed her.

I didn't hear the car pull up behind me until I heard the door slam shut. I whirled around prepared to protect myself no matter what, with whatever power I could muster.

~ ~ ~

I guzzled the bottle of water Jake handed me as he turned the heat on in the car. The coolness of the morning along with the relief from seeing Jake left me shaking involuntarily.

Or, maybe it was the drugs?

He pulled the car into an alley. "I've been lookin' for you everywhere. I showed up at the house this morning and your sister said somethin' terrible happened. She's worried about you."

I took another drink of water. I couldn't get enough. "Is she okay?"

"Yeah, but she said you and Aiden got into a fight about what happened at the meetin' and then you disappeared. She said Aiden told her you ran away, but it didn't sound like you to up and leave without tellin' her."

Of course, Aiden had said that. That was his plan. Kory probably had no idea I'd been in the hospital.

"I need to get to the coast," I said.

"The coast? Why?" Jake looked incredulous.

"I have a friend there that can help. Please, Jake, there is so much more going on than you know. I didn't run away. As a matter of fact, I woke up in a hospital and Aiden knew I was there."

After much prodding, Jake agreed to drive me to the coast without me using the power to convince him. I told him we could stay in Iris' home if he would drive to Locklyn. He wanted to know the real story; the truth about what happened last night and where I'd been. Was his disillusionment in the great Aiden growing?

I told him about feeling weird during the meeting and about my fight with Aiden, leaving out the tiny detail that Aiden was possessed by a demon and that it was Calder's voice that had brought me out of my apparent drug induced stupor. I told him about D'Netta saying I tested positive for drugs.

"But you've never done drugs? Ever?" Jake asked, a little too unconvinced.

"No, I haven't. But she said I tested positive. I'm thinking someone must have drugged me yesterday, although I'm not sure when – maybe it was in my food."

Suddenly Jake slammed his fist into the steering wheel and breathed a word under his breath.

"Jake, what is it? What's wrong?"

"I think I know who drugged you."

"Who?"

Jake turned his head slightly and I could see his eyes welling up with tears.

"Me."

Thinking I heard him wrong and hoping I had, I asked, "What?"

"When I showed up before the meeting I ran into Aiden as I was passin' the kitchen headed to the back door. He called me into the kitchen to talk, that's why I was fifteen minutes late gettin' there. He was makin' iced coffee for himself and Rachel and asked if I wanted some. I told him no, I don't usually drink coffee in the evenin'. And he said you love it, especially flavored coffees."

He shook his head and continued, "He said he knew you and I had been spendin' a lot of time together and he thought that was great, but I needed to watch out. That you weren't comin' around to the principles of the Order and that you might be planting seeds in the minds of other members, including your mom and sister. He warned me not to fall for anything you had to say about the Order or your beliefs otherwise. But, that conversation flagged somethin' in me. It told me Aiden was insecure around you. He was worried you would influence the members and those closest to you. He handed me that coffee and told me to take it to you because you would love it. But, I had better not say it was from him because you would probably dump it on the floor. He knew I was meetin' you."

We both sat quietly, contemplating what this meant. Aiden had drugged me. He'd used Jake to get to me. That's why I couldn't focus enough to even fight him last night.

"It wasn't your fault, Jake. He used you. He's deceptive and evil and he's got my mother and sister believing in him."

"Last night was strange too. We had several visitors there and at the end of the meetin', Aiden asked your mother and sister to join him on stage. The three of them stood on stage holdin' hands and then Aiden asked the visitors to join the Order of Greatness. Right then. The amazing thing was all twelve visitors joined last night and these aren't just anyone. He introduced me to each one. We're talkin' influential and powerful business people – wealthy people – and they joined without a second thought."

I was right. Aiden was using Rachel's Elemental energy, and probably Kory's too, to recruit for the Order.

"Aiden almost killed me last night and Rachel walked out of the room and all but shut the door. Why would she do that? Why wouldn't she protect me?" My eyes filled with tears as Jake wrapped his free arm around my shoulder and pulled me next to him.

We drove a long time like that.

CHAPTER TWENTY-NINE

When we finally reached the coast, Jake wanted to know where to meet my friend. The answer "I don't know" was met by a scowl, but he followed me down to the beach anyway. We were still a few hours from Locklyn, but the sooner I could summon Calder, the better. I didn't have the shell necklace, so all I could do was hope. Even with the blue stones connecting our souls.

In a secluded area of the beach, I found the prettiest shells to hopefully summon Calder to me. Jake sat down on a rock, watching me, probably wondering if Aiden had pushed me towards insanity. We would soon see.

Kicking off my shoes, I walked a few feet into the ocean with the material of my jeans absorbing the warm saltwater, weighing me down. Raising my hands into the air with my shell offering, I repeated Rachel's words.

"From the depths below and the sky above, bring me the one to train the young."

I stood motionless with only the waves crashing around me. Finally, I screamed at the top of my lungs.

"CALDER!"

I waited another long minute, and then screamed his name again. My only answer came in the crashing of waves and seagulls crying out as they passed. But no supernatural being. No angel or man. No Calder. Not even so much as a Krakken.

My face grew hot as I dropped my arms and headed back to Jake. I stared hard at the sand, so he wouldn't witness the hot tears streaming down my cheeks. Without help, how could I possibly stop Aiden and the Order? How could I save Kory? A few feet from Jake I slowed and looked up at him, expecting him to meet my pitiful gaze. Except he wasn't looking at me at all. His mouth was wide open as he slowly began to stand on the rock, staring past me. I whirled around and came face to face with Calder, my head almost bumping into his shoulder. Again, his chest was bare, but I didn't care. He was here, and he could help me.

"My little, Ava Grace, why are you screaming for me?" He half grinned and my knees almost buckled. Come on, Ava.

"Calder, something horrible has happened. Aiden Blake is possessed by the demon. He almost killed me last night."

The expression on Calder's face never changed. He glanced up at Jake who moved closer to me. "Who is your friend?"

"Not really the time for introductions," I said, waving my hand. When both men stared at me, I gave in. "Calder, this is my friend, Jake Henderson. Jake, this is my, err, friend, Calder."

"Calder doesn't have a last name?" Jake asked.

Calder grunted, and with one look dismissed Jake. He frowned, and a drop of sea water dropped from his hair and ran down his face. "Aiden Blake is Rachel's fiancé. Where is she?" He asked, focusing back on why he was here.

How could I tell him my mother had left me at the mercy of a possessed man, a demon? How could I tell him I had no idea if Rachel was for us…or against us? Seeming to sense that I was struggling for the words to say, Calder cradled my head in his hands. At first, I thought it was a sweet gesture as he ran his thumbs over my temples, until I realized last night's adventures were playing through my mind's eye. Calder was accessing my memories. The last memory before he let go was Jake kissing the top of my head in the car. Calder dropped his hands and glanced back and forth from me to Jake.

"This demon has power over Rachel and Kory because of the trinket, the bracelet. You had one, too. You sensed its evil subconsciously and I helped you destroy it. You're more powerful than the other two. With you, it's instinct. But," he took a deep breath, "the demon has exploited your weakness. He knows you still haven't forgiven Rachel for giving you to Iris. He's used that to separate you."

Jake interrupted, "What demon? What are you two talking about?"

Jake was still in the dark about who I truly was. Maybe that made two of us.

"Jake, Aiden isn't just evil," I said, choosing my words carefully. Jake was Aiden's protégé after all, and possibly the next leader of the Order of Greatness.

"He is possessed by a demon or rather precisely, he has become the demon. Rachel, Kory, and I are part of a group of women called Elementals, what men referred to as Sirens. We were chosen by God to root out the demons and destroy them. It's also why we were attacked last night at the greenhouse."

"The problem with this demon," Calder said, "is he already knew about the Elementals and targeted them right away. By giving them a cursed object, he could render them powerless against him. The only way to do that was to get close to them through Rachel."

Jake ran his hand through his hair. "He drugged Ava last night. He could've killed her. What do we do?"

Calder shook his head. "He wants to do more than kill. He wants to take their power and use it for himself. He would be able to attract the masses into his cult and easily kill his opposition." He pulled the small scroll I'd found in the Meeting room from his pocket.

"This," he continued, unraveling the parchment. "This paper isn't just a letter in code as you suspected. According to my source, this is an ancient language. Well, ancient for you, I suppose." Calder smiled.

"It is written in a Celtic script known as Ogham. It may even be older than Ogham, from the continental Celtic language, a language that is now extinct. These markings represent their tree alphabet. It is a covenant between the demon, Elhath, and the elders of the Order of Greatness. Apparently, this Order goes back much further than I thought. Elhath is a powerful demon who both influences and possesses. He is not always in possession of the Leader. He can move around – invisibly influencing others – until he needs the Leader again. Sometimes he will leave behind a foul stench, insects, or a substance, but for the most part, nothing at all. We can't do anything except prepare for the next attack. As long as Rachel and Kory are under his power, they can't break free long enough to fight him. And if he senses he is losing control of them, he may kill them outright."

I thought about the black sludge in the office fireplace and the flies in the kitchen window. "Aiden looked tired yesterday morning. The demon – this Elhath – must have left Aiden's body for a short while to move around Carey House. But if that's true, who did it influence, and why?"

Jake reached for the scroll and Calder handed it to him after a moment of hesitation. Jake nodded his head as he studied the symbols. "There are Ogham stones inside Carey House. One's in Aiden's office and a larger one in the Meeting room. I'm pretty sure these symbols match."

"The Elders of the Order must have copied the covenant onto parchment. The Ogham stones may very well help to empower Elhath and that's why they've been moved from their native home," Calder said.

"How can we beat this Elhath? Is there a weapon?" Jake asked.

Calder nodded towards me. "She's the weapon."

"Okay," Jake said slowly, not totally convinced of my weaponry skills. "Is there a tangible weapon I could use? We saw somethin' last night, but it went through us. Is there somethin' I can use that will stop that? To help me get in there and save Rachel and Kory?"

Calder considered his words. "I may be able to craft something with help from Iris' stones. I'll see what I can do."

I placed my hand on Calder's chest. "Calder, please. There has to be a way to get to them, to save them."

He covered my hand with his and slowly shook his head. "I can't do anything from here. I cannot go to Carey House again with limited power. This demon is clever enough to know not to come to the coast."

With a glance toward Jake, Calder led me out into the ocean a few feet. I leaned my head onto his shoulder, his breath on my hair. I allowed myself to let down the invisible barrier that separated us. My heart filled with hopelessness and frustration. Calder's feelings.

"I'm not afraid anymore. Iris told me I've already won this battle," I said as I looked up into Calder's face and watched him smile at the mention of Iris' name. "Jake and I can go, but I don't know what to do," I whispered.

"You know what to do, what has to be done. Get the bracelets off the girls to break his hold. When all is said and done, come back to the coast and call for me. In the meantime, I will try to find another way to come to you. Remember who you are. While you're worried, Ava, God is already there."

He ran his hand through my hair and smiled. "You remind me so much of Iris. She defeated many demons in her lifetime without the help of two other Brewer women. You can, too. And just like Iris, I'll be here waiting for you." He winked and then kissed my forehead. "No matter how many boys you choose to spend your time with."

I watched him walk out into the ocean, barely aware that Jake now stood at my side. "What is he?"

"He's an angel." I shook my head not sure where that thought came from. "No, I don't know what he is, but he will help us."

CHAPTER THIRTY

It was getting late, so we decided to sleep on the beach. Jake was tired from driving and I still hadn't recovered from the last twenty-four hours, so when he suggested we use the two blankets from his trunk, I almost jumped for joy. We spread one onto the sand near the dunes and used the other as a cover after making a small fire at my insistence to keep the sand crabs and other beach creatures at bay. Hopefully, we were far enough away from the beach houses that no one would see us and call the authorities. Jake held me close but didn't try anything. Which in and of itself could have been disappointing, except I felt like Calder could see us.

As I nestled into Jake's arms and closed my eyes, Jake whispered in my ear, "What's with you and that Calder?"

I turned over onto my back and faced him. Jake pushed himself up onto his elbow. I could see his green eyes flickering in the moonlight. "Have you ever heard of a Siren? Like the legend of Sirens?"

"Yeah, the women who would derail men on ships. Like in The Odyssey."

"Exactly, the stories got sleazy and made them to be evil, but in reality, they were women chosen by God to locate a demon using their attractiveness. Eventually the Siren, who we call Elemental, would lure the demon close enough to kill it."

Jake ran his finger over my shoulder, sending goosebumps down my arms. "So, you lure men to find out which one is a demon? How do you know?"

"Calder said demons love mortal women. In ancient times, the fallen angels were known to mate with human women and father an entire race of creatures called Nephilim. But, anyway, I can feel when evil is close, and I start having visions and hearing voices. Sometimes they're horrible."

"Where does Calder fit in?" Jake asked, lying down on his arm stretching out.

"I'm not sure. He comes out of the sea. Rachel summoned him when we were in North Carolina. He knew my aunt, too." I decided not to mention the love between Iris and Calder or the blue stone. "I know sometimes I can feel what he is feeling. Rachel said he is here to help all the Elementals defeat demons, but he can only come so far inland. I don't know what Calder really is, but I do know we can trust him." I turned over onto my side and closed my eyes. Tomorrow we would drive to Locklyn to rest and then start the drive back to Carey House.

But Jake didn't go to sleep. He wasn't done on the whole Calder thing. "So, he is just a creature from the sea in the form of a man." I wasn't sure if that was supposed to be a question or a statement.

I exhaled a little too loudly, unsure why I felt defensive. "I told you. I don't know what Calder really is, but you don't have to make him sound like Lochness of the Lake."

Jake pulled me closer. "Why are you gettin' so defensive?" He whispered into my ear.

I pulled away and this time sat up, turning to see his face again. "Why are you so jealous?" I retorted.

"Jealous?" Jake jumped off the blanket and stood in front of me, his cheeks red. "How is it jealousy when I'm askin' you about a man you're puttin' all your trust in? A man who's not even human. A man I'm not even to question?" He walked a few feet away, got a second wind, and pointed his finger at me. "I thought you were smart and clever. I never saw you fallin' so blindly for some guy, or whatever he is, like your mom did with Aiden."

I glared at him. "Or like you, following Aiden so blindly in the Order doing his every bidding?" He'd fallen for Aiden's lies just as much as Rachel had. Even worse, Aiden was grooming him to lead the Order one day. Essentially all of the members of the Order believed everything out of the mouth of the demon.

Jake glared out at the ocean, the apparent source of his conflict.

I wanted to argue with him, tell him Calder was born this way. I wasn't sure how I knew that, but I did. And part of him was human.

Let it go, Ava, I told myself. Jake is not the enemy. As a matter of fact, he's my only friend and ally.

I moved off the blanket. As I came close to him, Jake eyed me suspiciously, probably wondering if I was using my abilities on him. I put my hands up in a gesture of surrender and leaned into him, laying my head on his chest. Through his shirt I could feel the thumping of his heart.

"I'm sorry, Jake."

After a moment of hesitation, he wrapped his arms around me and breathed a sigh. We were fighting for the same team so why did I feel as if one of us was going to lose?

I looked up at Jake's face and was met with the scent of saltwater and sand from his skin. He was still staring out into the ocean, jaw clenched. Impulsively, I kissed his clenched jaw slowly and ran my finger over the side of his face. He drew back a moment, his mouth forming a silent question. Then he kissed me hard, almost awkwardly. I shut out the screams in my head telling me not here, not now, not the time.

Not with Jake.

He picked me up and I wrapped my legs around him as he carried me over to our blankets. When he dropped to his knees, I held on tighter afraid he would drop me, but he lowered us onto the blanket in perfect control. I had underestimated Jake's strength for a teenage boy. As he kissed my neck, I arched my back and turned towards the ocean.

Then my heart broke.

I felt my insides tear in two. I suddenly wanted to cry.

"Jake. Jake, stop." He raised his eyes to meet mine and I could see passion burning behind them.

"What's wrong?" He breathed heavily.

"I, I don't know. This isn't the right time," I stammered, but I couldn't help it. I was torn. My heart was heavy and sad while my body burned for Jake. Were these my emotions or Calder's? I sat up and shook my head.

Jake moved onto his knees and stared hard at the rumpled blanket. "Is it him?" He asked without looking up.

"I don't know," I said as I laid down on the blanket, facing the ocean while silent tears ran down my face. Jake left the blankets and walked down the beach some distance. When he came back, I had almost cried myself to sleep.

He snuggled behind me under the blanket, pulling me close. "I want you to know that I may not be immortal or perfect or a supernatural being. But, I would die for you, Ava." He turned his mouth closer to my ear.

"And more importantly, I'd live for you."

CHAPTER THIRTY-ONE

The next morning, we found a restaurant and while Jake bought breakfast, I cleaned up in the bathroom as best I could. I still felt a mess, but less nasty. Once in the car, I wolfed down my ham and cheese croissant and caramel mocha latte. I hadn't eaten since before the meeting at Carey House.

I used Jake's phone to call Kory's number. It went straight to voicemail. Of course, Aiden may have taken it from her. Jake said he had three missed calls from Aiden and a message asking him where he was, so I decided it probably wouldn't be the best idea to leave her a message just in case. Jake messaged Aiden back that he was staying with a friend for a few days, a message he also sent to his uncle. Jake was quiet as he drove, however, the silence didn't bother me like I thought it would. I needed to get into Carey House and get Kory. We needed a plan.

I shut my eyes and silently prayed for the first time in a while. *God, I'm sorry I haven't talked to you in a while, but you know what is happening. You know about Aiden and the demon and the Order...all of it. You know what I don't. Please help me to save my sister and Rachel with the ability you gave me. Or, send me Calder or someone who can help me. I don't know if I can do this alone and there is a lot to lose. Thank you.*

"While you were in the bathroom, I Googled Nephilim," Jake said.

I started at his voice. "What? Why?"

Why were we still on this? We had other things to worry about than Calder's origins.

"It brought up sites stating that Nephilim in the Bible were the children of mortal women and fallen angels. It says in the Bible in the book of Genesis, they were heroes of old. In the book of Numbers, it says they were giants. At any rate, they were a sight to behold, far better than mortal men or women."

"I'm not sure what you're getting at, Jake. I only mentioned the Nephilim to show you that demons are already attracted to human women. The Sirens and Elementals just have a little extra IT."

"Because the more I think about it, the more I believe Calder may be one," Jake said.

"If we survive this battle with the demon, I'll ask Calder about it, okay? We have more important things to worry about than who his parents are right now. Like how to make Rachel and Kory see that Aiden is the very demon we've been looking for."

Jake asked, "What time does the last member usually leave from helping around the house?"

"Maybe around seven, but I've seen you there past nine. Martha was usually there until dusk, but she's gone now."

"What do you mean gone?"

"Aiden said that Martha had decided to go back to Ireland, but she'd stopped me in the kitchen the night before and warned me about bad spirits in the house. She was terrified of something or someone."

Jake shook his head. "He didn't say anything to me about Martha. I would've thought he'd made a big deal out of that. Martha's been with him from the beginning, even before Roger and Julia joined. Well, Aiden doesn't know I'm with you. I'll go to the front door and talk to Aiden and maybe you can slip in the back."

The plan sounded perfect. If I could get in and get to Kory first, she could help me convince Rachel. At the very least remove the bracelet keeping Aiden's hold over her. It still hurt to think back to that night, seeing her back out of the room when Aiden told her to. And according to Jake, Kory believed Aiden's lie that I had run away even though she thought it sounded off.

I turned towards the window and closed my eyes. I needed to rest before battle.

~ ~ ~

Iris' house was still locked up tight when Jake and I opened the door.

"Do you still want to see Pastor Simms while you're here?" Jake asked.

"Yeah, of course. We need all the help we can get. I just need a couple of hours to rest. I definitely need a shower." I tugged on my filthy blouse as I made my way to my bedroom. Unfortunately, all my clothes were at Carey House. I checked Kory's room, but to no avail. The girl had taken every stitch of her overstuffed closet. I slipped into Iris' bedroom. Thank God, Aiden hadn't sent any members to clean out the rooms for guests yet. I opened Iris' closet and ran my hand through her wardrobe. Most of it were outfits a girl my age would never wear, but then I spied a familiar dark blue maxi-dress. The one I'd seen her wearing in my vision of Iris and Calder. It was a size small.

Iris kept two-piece swimsuits in her top dresser drawer. Of course, she would. Iris was a beautiful Siren-ish woman.

I took a quick shower and dressed, replacing my underwear with the swimsuit under the dress. It took several minutes to clean my flats from the dried mud.

I walked into the kitchen to find Jake making a can of turkey chili.

"Feel better?" He asked.

"Definitely," I answered, braiding my damp hair.

He pointed to the saucepot on the stove. "It's the only thing I could find to eat."

"We cleaned out everything else except for the canned food. I don't care. It smells delicious." I picked up the cordless phone from the charger and went back in the living room to find Pastor Simms' phone number. The problem with using cell phones constantly is never memorizing a number. The end table held Iris' little blue book, chock full of phone numbers, addresses, and passwords. Pastor Simms answered on the second ring.

"Ava! It's so good to hear from you! Although it's a little early," Pastor Simms' deep voice tested the volume control on the phone. I glanced at the clock on the wall. It was almost eleven.

"Thanks. I'm actually here in Locklyn and was hoping I could come by the church and talk to you." When Pastor Simms hesitated, I continued, "I'm in trouble."

"What kind of trouble?"

"It's Aiden, Rachel's fiancé. He's not who everyone thinks he is. Can I come by the church this morning or early afternoon? I'm only in town a little while."

"Sure. Would one be alright? I have a meeting at eleven-thirty about some business and I would love to pick up our conversation from before about Aiden and this Order of Greatness. I think they are far more than they seem."

I agreed and hung up the phone just as Jake set my bowl of chili down on the coffee table. "Did he say he'd meet us?" He asked, digging into his lunch.

"Yes, at one o'clock. But, he sounded odd."

"What do you mean?"

"I don't know. Pastor Simms has always had a big personality, but it seemed like he knew more about the Order since I left for West Virginia. He said he couldn't wait to talk with me about Aiden and the Order. Maybe it's just me. Too much to think about." I took a bite of chili. It tasted amazing. I went in for a second bite when the doorbell rang. Jake and I jumped at the sound.

I peeked through the front window blinds to see Kory's friend, Dillon standing on the front porch. He pushed his cap back away from his eyes when I opened the door, clearly happy to see me.

"Hey, A! Is Kory home?" Dillon greeted me with his version of my nickname. It used to irritate me, but today it sounded nice to have someone care enough to give me a moniker.

"Um, no. How did you know I was here?" I asked, looking up and down the street for an Aiden-spy.

"I saw the car with West Virginia tags. Knew it was you two. Who else could it be?" He stared past me as Jake came to stand at my shoulder.

"Actually," I said, "Kory didn't come with me. My friend Jake and I took a road trip."

The guys made head motions at one another which I guess was one step higher in respect than a grunt. "Do you want to come in? I'm going to stop and say hi to Pastor Simms before we leave."

Dillon kept his eyes on Jake as he answered, "No, that's okay. Just tell Kory I stopped by and asked about her."

After I shut the door, Jake whispered as if Dillon possessed supernatural hearing, "Wow. He's really into your sister."

"I know. He's had a crush on her forever." As I sat down to finish lunch, a thought occurred to me. "Do you think we should have told him about Aiden and Carey House? I know it sounds incredible, but maybe he could help somehow. At the very least, get Kory to safety if we can't."

Jake didn't question me about the 'if we can't' statement. "He'd think we're crazy. What if he calls Kory and tells her we're here?"

"We'll be long gone by the time the Order sends someone. Aiden might not send anyone at all. He wanted me to run away. Maybe he would expect me to live here in peace and never bother them again. You know, that was the choice I was given just a couple of weeks ago that I could either follow my sister to Webster Mills or live here by myself. Just the other day, Aiden offered me this house, so I could finish my senior year here. Maybe I should call Aiden and take him up on the offer."

Jake laughed at my dry sense of humor. But, even as I said the words, I didn't believe them. Aiden wanted me gone. For good.

"I wanted to tell Freya everything. She's my best friend, but after what happened at the house, I'd only put her in danger. She's simply another person they could use to hurt me."

"No, it's probably best if we do this alone. I don't wanna to see anyone get hurt," Jake said, and then added quietly, "especially you."

After I ate, I went and laid down for a quick nap on my bed. I was what Iris would've called "bone tired." Every part of me still ached even after my Elemental powers had healed my wounds.

Jake knocked softly on the open door. "Can I lay down with you? Promise, no kissing," he smiled.

I motioned for him to come over and as he slid next to me and wrapped his arms around me, my body started to relax.

"When we were on the beach last night, you accused me of followin' Aiden blindly. You were right," he whispered into my ear. "Since my parents died, I've felt like I didn't matter to anyone. Even my uncle is busy with his own life. Aiden and I grew up a lot alike. He was the first one to give me a chance, to rely on me to get stuff done, just like Mr. Carey did for him. Now the Elders ask my opinion on matters. They take my advice. No one's ever done that before."

He moved his hand up to his eyes and I realized he was wiping away tears. I squeezed his arm. He continued, "But maybe I feel that way because I'd lost my self-worth when Mom and Dad died. Since I've been around you I feel a confidence, an inner strength I never knew I had. Maybe that's what sets me apart from Aiden." He squeezed me tighter and kissed my hair before falling to sleep.

According to my Iris-vision, my strength was on the other side of my fear. I didn't feel fear anymore, but I didn't feel strength either. Not yet. At least, we were both safe for now.

I hugged Jake's arms tightly as I drifted off to sleep.

~ ~ ~

Sweet Hills Baptist Church was the subject of many paintings, I was sure of it. The little white church sat nestled under trees with its steeple so close to the branches that the congregation had to pay for regular tree trimming services. As we drove past the split rail fence, Jake let out a low whistle.

"How old is this place?" He asked.

"I think the building was erected in the 1940s. The recreation building is over that hill. It's a bit newer. I think the church owns eighty acres of land here," I answered, as I pointed to Pastor Simms' Expedition, parked to the right of the church, in his reserved spot. The main parking lot was located around back, but Jake pulled up and parked behind Pastor Simms' truck.

The church doors were locked, so we knocked and waited. The church office was located on the second floor above the foyer. After a few minutes, Jake knocked again, much harder this time.

"If he's in his study, he'll have a difficult time hearing us."

"Yeah, but, he's expectin' us, remember?" Jake said, as he stepped off the stoop and peered up at the second-floor window. After a few more minutes of waiting, we decided to walk around to the side door that led to the kitchen area. The screen door was shut but unlocked. The kitchen door itself stood wide open.

"Bizarre," I mumbled under my breath. The front doors were locked up tight, but the side door was propped open by a round stone.

"Pastor Simms?" I called out. No answer. Jake followed me through the kitchen and dining areas to the sanctuary. We walked down the main aisle and into the foyer. "Pastor Simms?" I called again up the stairwell.

Jake and I stared at each other. Neither one of us wanted to say it, but what if the Order had come to Locklyn? I placed my foot on the first step, but Jake motioned for me to wait. He stepped in front of me as we climbed the carpeted stairs to the second floor.

The small window let in enough light that Jake and I could see that the front office was neat and empty. The door that led to Pastor Simms' study was closed. I knocked quietly on the old wooden door. "Pastor Simms? It's Ava. We had an appointment at one o'clock?"

Not a sound came through the door.

Jake turned the knob and the door opened easily. As he pushed the door wide, we stood aghast, neither one of us spoke.

Pastor Simms lay face down on his desk. A large round stone painted red jutted out from his skull at an odd angle. I covered my mouth as I realized the stone wasn't painted at all. Blood was everywhere. I backed away into the office. I needed air. I ran down the stairs and through the sanctuary to the back door. I barely made it to the grass before I vomited.

A few minutes later, Jake joined me. His face twisted between shock and fear. "We have to call the police," he said.

"They'll want to know why we're here. What if they think we did it?" I asked, as I looked around at the witnessing trees.

Jake bent over with his hands on his knees as he tossed a small black book down on the ground between his feet. "I went in his office and found this planner. I flipped to this week. Guess what it says?" He asked. He still had his head down. I assumed to keep from gagging. I stepped closer. The black book appeared to have drops of blood on it.

"Is that blood?" I asked as I backed away again.

Jake ignored the question as he opened the book. "Pastor Simms had a meetin' scheduled with Roger Carter this mornin' at eleven-thirty."

"He said he had a meeting at eleven-thirty to wrap up some business," I said. I could barely get the words out. "What would Roger want with Pastor Simms?" I asked, my voice catching in my throat.

"How would we find out?" He stood up and stared expressionless into the trees. "I think you're right though. If we call the cops, they'll take us in for questioning. If we don't…our fingerprints are everywhere inside."

"If Roger knew Pastor Simms was meeting with me, then he could have set this up. Someone propped the side door open. Does it say anything else in his planner, about maybe meeting with Aiden last week regarding property deals?"

Jake thumbed back through the planner. I bit my tongue from pointing out the streak of blood on the back of his hand. "Here we go. Last Wednesday, Aiden requested to meet with the Pastor about usin' the recreation building. Why would he do that?"

"Aiden said he wanted to expand the Order's territory into North Carolina, and Locklyn specifically, since it's near the tourist towns and beaches. I know the church sometimes rents out the recreation building to groups for events. Maybe Aiden wanted to use it for the Order." A thought occurred to me. "Oh my God."

"What?"

"I told you Aiden tried to talk me into returning to Locklyn to finish my senior year. Well, I made him promise if I did return that the Order could not do any business in town. And he said that the Order had business outside of city limits, but that he could promise me that the Order would stay out of the town. I bet he was talking about this place. It's outside city limits, secluded, and large enough to build on."

I took a deep breath. Pastor Simms would have never let the Order of Greatness use the church's property for their indoctrination pursuits. If anyone would have stood up to Aiden, it would've been Pastor Simms. But, did Roger or someone from the Order, kill him?

I asked for Jake's cell phone, but before I could Google the number to the Locklyn Police Department, the phone rang. Roger Carter's name appeared. I thrust the phone towards Jake. It rang four times and then went to voicemail. Roger didn't leave a message.

Instead, a text message popped up on the phone.

I KNOW YOU ARE HANGING WITH FRIENDS THE NEXT FEW DAYS, BUT NEED YOU TO CALL.

All caps. An urgent message from an Elder of the Order. I could see Jake wrestling with what to do next.

"We need to call the police, Jake. Even if they question us, we have no motive."

"But if Roger sent this, then doesn't it mean, he's probably home in Webster Mills? If that's true, then he couldn't have killed Pastor Simms."

"It doesn't mean someone else from the Order didn't kill him. Or, for all we know, he could be calling you from somewhere in Locklyn, or up the road." Jake and I stared at each other. He didn't want to believe the Order could be involved in something as heinous as murder.

"If the Order did kill your Pastor, then we can believe they will kill your mother and sister if necessary."

Without a word, we got back into Jake's car with Pastor Simms' book and headed to West Virginia. If we survived battling the demon and the Order while saving my mother and sister, then we would talk to the police.

If we survived.

~ ~ ~

Before we left the area, I made Jake stop at the beach one more time. If Aiden did destroy the pond, then this was my last chance to recharge using the ocean as a resource. I only had a few minutes, so I kicked off my flats and walked into the water, careful to pull my dress up so it wouldn't get wet.

A dark shadow suddenly emerged in front of me and I turned around to face Calder.

"I'm glad you came to the ocean. I'm still trying to find a way to join you, but I have something. Can you meet me at the caves?" He asked.

"Of course, but things are a lot more serious now. The Order of Greatness means business. I think they murdered the pastor at Sweet Hills Baptist. Most likely because he refused to sell the property."

Calder frowned and then nodded his head. "Come to the caves quickly then."

I made Jake wait outside the caves as I ventured in. Calder stood waiting for me with his hands behind his back. "Ava, if I can get to you I will, but this may help."

From behind his back he pulled out an ornate dagger, probably close to twelve inches long. The handle was encrusted in jewels of all kinds –

sapphire, emerald, ruby, diamond – that I was pretty sure were genuine. I took it from him and held it up to the sunlight pouring in from the cave's entrance. It gleamed beautifully. At the end of the handle encased in gold was one of Iris' quartz stones.

"You made this?" I asked. Only a supernatural being could have crafted something so exquisite in less than a day.

"With help, yes. If the demon materializes into its original form, this will help you kill it. You'll need to get close to it, so be careful. Just remember, it doesn't replace your God-given abilities. It's only to help you."

"A double-edged sword," I whispered.

"Well, a double-edged dagger," Calder smiled as he touched my braid that had fallen loose on my shoulder.

I nodded my head and then gave Calder a quick kiss on the cheek before heading back to Jake's car.

With the dagger by my side, I finally felt stronger.

CHAPTER THIRTY-TWO

J ake stopped his car a good way from the house so as not to be seen. I
ran behind the trees on the edge of the woods around back to the
greenhouse and waited. My feet were killing me. I'd been wearing these
flats for three days straight. I crouched down just inside the greenhouse door
and listened for Jake's car as I adjusted my make-shift sword belt. Jake had
tied his belt around me and looped it in such a way that it held the dagger
close to my hip. Without a sheath on the blade, I had to be careful that I
didn't stab myself. As I balanced in a squat, my hand brushed over
something on the floor. Plastic. I picked it up and held it in front of the
window.

I could barely make out the two pictures. Martha's family pictures. I
dropped them on the floor as I realized the wetness on my fingers was blood.
Martha had never left the estate. Afraid to search the greenhouse only to
find Martha's body, I took my chances and ran to the back of the house.

I heard Jake's car roll up to the front and less than thirty seconds later
heard him slam the door. I waited another minute to make sure he'd been
able to get someone, hopefully Aiden, to come to the front door. I couldn't

see him from the back of the house, so I could only hope he was inside. Taking one last look at the windows above searching for movement, I sprinted to the back door. Thank God it wasn't locked yet. I opened it slightly and listened. There were muffled voices from somewhere near the front of the house.

I shut the door quietly behind me and slipped along the wall in the dining room. I glanced into the kitchen. It was empty. I darted to the other side of the dining room wall and peeked around the doorway. Aiden was standing at the front door talking to Jake. I couldn't hear the words since it was on the opposite end of the Great Hall. I pulled my head back just in time as Aiden shut the front door and he and Jake headed for the smaller hallway. Jake must have convinced him to talk in his office. Perfect, I thought. If they shut the door, I could easily slip thru the hall and up the stairs to Kory's room.

Instead they stopped in front of the small hallway.

"Jake, I don't know why you are lying to me," Aiden's voice raised enough that I could hear. "Is it because of Ava? She's going to lead you astray. She's lost, not to mention delusional and on drugs. She never wanted to come here in the first place. Since she's been here, she has tried to turn both her mother and Kory against me and the Order. Do you know that she attacked D'Netta?" Aiden placed his hand on Jake's shoulder.

I held my breath.

Jake was quiet for a moment and I wondered if he would tell all, point me out to Aiden and leave me to confront the monster myself.

"There's no reason to question my loyalty, Aiden. Have I not been here every day, learning from you, absorbing your knowledge? I've poured sweat and blood into the Order, and I would never give that up over some brat-faced girl."

Aiden seemed pleased with his answer and patted Jake on the shoulder. The two of them disappeared into the smaller hall headed for Aiden's office.

I didn't want to take the time to consider Jake's harsh words and prayed he was still actually on my team, so when I heard the office door shut, I took off my shoes and ran as fast as I could across the Great Hall. I hit the stairs two at a time until I reached the second floor before I heard a crash. It had come from the smaller hallway corridor. Fear started to overwhelm me, but I pushed it back. Had something gone wrong? I needed to get to Kory now.

I rounded the corner and practically flew up the little steps to the third floor. I didn't bother knocking on Kory's door, but flung it open and ran in. Kory laid across her bed with her tablet.

"Where have you been? Dillon said he saw you and Jake at home in Locklyn," she hissed at me. I couldn't tell if she was mad at me or didn't want anyone to hear.

"Well, I sure didn't run away despite rumors you may have heard," I said sarcastically as I grabbed her arm. "Come on, we've got to get out of here."

"Stop, Ava. What are you doing?" She protested more as I pulled her off the bed. I grabbed the charm bracelet on her wrist and yanked as hard as I could. The bracelet gave, and the charms and beads rolled all over the floor. Kory covered her mouth to keep from screaming at me.

"Listen to me, Kory. Aiden is possessed with the demon we've been looking for. That bracelet he gave us included a charm that made him immune to our powers, and even worse, put him in control over us. He's blinded us, Kory. He's blinded our mother." Kory removed her hand from her mouth.

"Are you sure?"

I nodded. "I verified it with Calder last night."

She looked around the room as if seeing everything for the first time. "We need to get Mom and get out of here. She went down to Aiden's office to talk to him about you a little while ago. Oh, and Dillon is here somewhere too. He flew in this afternoon."

"Dillon?" I asked. "Why is he here? I just saw him this morning."

Kory slipped her Toms on with lightning fast speed. "He said Aiden called him and asked him to come up and keep me company with you gone. Roger picked him up from the airport this afternoon."

Everything began to click into place. I'd looked for an Aiden-spy and he'd stood on my front porch this morning. Maybe Roger hadn't been in Webster Mills. If Aiden got to Dillon, then maybe the foolish boy had killed Pastor Simms. I decided not to tell Kory about the crash I heard or about Pastor Simms. If Rachel was in the office and then Jake...

Kory and I made it down the stairs from the third floor to the second when I heard whispering coming from the den. When we got to the doorway, Julia was standing in the room with her arms raised and a white mist hovering above her. She was wearing a white robe with the same red symbols from the Meeting Room banners and the scroll.

Kory and I exchanged glances as we moved quietly into the room. We would have bypassed the den and went straight to Aiden's office except for the chanting. Julia chanted to the mist in a foreign language, probably the lost language Calder mentioned. The more she chanted the faster the mist seemed to swirl.

Was the mist a ghost or another demon? Kory waved at me. With Julia's back to us, Kory began mouthing words in my direction. I mouthed back the word, "What?"

She mouthed back, "I got this."

Before I could tell her no, Kory moved away from me and headed right for Julia. However, before she could touch her, Julia whirled around. The sweet woman from moving day was gone. Julia formed her mouth into a snarl and raised her hand to hit Kory. A burst of energy streamed from my sister's hand, knocking Julia over the couch and into the glass coffee table, shattering it into a million pieces. The mist dissipated.

Julia didn't move.

We both stared down at the dead woman. At least, she looked dead with her wide eyes staring blankly up at the ceiling, pieces of glass in her neck.

So much blood.

I positioned myself in front of Kory as we crept through the second floor. The house was eerily quiet. There was no way someone hadn't heard Julia crash through the glass coffee table. If the Elders could summon mists and apparitions, like Julia, then we had more than just the demon to fight. When we finally made it to the top of the stairs, we could see the Great

Hall. Neither Aiden, Rachel, nor Jake appeared. We still needed to find Rachel and get out of the house and away from Aiden and the Order.

"No matter what happens, stay with me, but if things look bad, then you get outside. Jake's car is parked right out front and he always leaves the keys in the floorboard." Kory nodded and squeezed my arm, but before I could touch her, a large hand grabbed my sister's face and pulled her backwards, almost knocking me down the marble steps.

I grabbed the bannister and turned around to see Roger standing several feet away with his strong arm wrapped around Kory's neck. He glared at me in contempt as he continued to squeeze. Kory whimpered, her arm outstretched in my direction.

"Roger, don't. Please," I pleaded.

The older man's lips curled in a lopsided smile. "You've tried to tear down something much older than you, little girl," he growled. "Aiden thought he needed you three, but he only needs Elhath. This ends here." He squeezed harder and Kory's eyes grew wide as she gasped for air and kicked her legs.

"This is your last chance. Take your sister and leave. Go back to your little house and never come near the Order again." He squeezed Kory's neck tighter.

I put my hand up. "I can't leave without our mother. Where is she?"

The old man smirked. "Your mother doesn't want you. She never has. It was Aiden who convinced her to bring you here, so he could use your powers for Elhath."

Kory's eyes began to roll up into her head as she fought to breathe.

"Last chance, girlie," Roger growled at me again.

Oh, God. He's going to break her neck.

Anger grew in the pit of my stomach, forcefully spewing out in the form of red energy. I hit Roger and Kory, knocking them both to the ground. Kory crawled quickly to me as I descended on Roger. In a moment, the spry old man was on his feet and punched me in the stomach. All the air left my lungs as I dropped to my knees. Before I could hit the ground, Roger pulled me up by my hair, his eyes as black as coal. I dangled a few inches from the ground, kicking him, but he didn't waver. I knew the only way to win this was to let go of the hand that held my braid and risk him pulling my hair out. I let go and gritted my teeth against the pain as I dug my fingernails into Roger's black eyes. The man screamed and dropped me.

But not before I'd managed to pluck one of his eyes from its socket.

Roger continued screaming as he bounced off the walls. I reached for Kory, but my sister ran past me and pushed Roger over the bannister. I heard his body hit the marble floor with a sickening thud.

I wiped my hands quickly on my jeans and tried to not to think about what was under my fingernails. Kory stood at the bannister and then turned to hug me. We both shook when she pointed to the blood running down my leg from the dagger's blade. With my adrenaline pumping, I must've fallen on the blade but never felt it. During my fight with Roger, the blade must've worked free again. It hung in its spot on my hip with the blood dripping onto the floor.

I mustered up a smile. "It's not as bad as it looks. Let's go."

If Rachel was still in Aiden's office, then another confrontation was imminent. We descended the marble stairs quietly and then sprinted across the hall to the smaller hallway corridor. The hall was super dark and super quiet. Unfortunately, the light switch was located on the other end of the hall past Aiden's office door. Not that we wanted to announce our arrival, but a little light would've been great. We both took a wall opposite each other and slowly made our way down the hall. The silence was deafening.

Until my foot caught something, and I fell forward. A small yelp escaped my lips as I took Kory down with me in a futile attempt to keep myself upright. As I scurried to keep quiet, I felt the object. Oh, God. It was a body. I ran my hand over the person's head and neck and knew at once it was Jake. Warm liquid filled my palm as I felt his hair. His breathing was slight. I turned him over onto his back and felt my way to his neck. His pulse was still there.

"It's Jake," I told Kory.

"Oh, God. Where's Mom?" Kory reached for my hand and I could barely make out her pointing to Aiden's office door. Light seeped out from the bottom and we made ourselves over to it, careful to maneuver around Jake.

My heart pounded hard and my chest tightened. Jake had risked all to help me and now he was lying unconscious on the floor, his head gushing blood. Fear and adrenaline were all I could feel now. Would our powers be enough to defeat Aiden? Would we be able to access them at the right time? I pushed the doubts out of my head and squeezed Kory's hand. *Oh God, where are you?*

Kory swung the door open.

~ ~ ~

The lamps with their red lampshades gave a sinister glow to the room. A grunt caused me to turn wildly to the left. Rachel sat behind the large oak desk; her mouth covered with duct tape and a hypodermic needle stuck out of her arm. What had Aiden done?

Kory immediately ran around to the side of the desk to get Rachel free. I stayed back, looking around the room. Where was Aiden?

"Ava, help me get her loose!" Kory was jerking the duct tape off Rachel's arms and legs as quickly as she could. She winced as she pulled the needle from Rachel's arm and tossed it on the desk. I went to the opposite side and started pulling on the duct tape. It was so much harder to pull off than I had seen in the movies. When Rachel got an arm free, she pulled the pieces from across her mouth.

"Where's Aiden? I think he may have killed Jake," Rachel slurred. Her eyes were wide and red from crying. A bruise graced her right cheek.

"I don't know, but we need to get out of here. Jake's in the hallway, but it's not good. Pull that bracelet off, too. That's how the demon can subdue our powers. Aiden is possessed by it. He blinded you."

Rachel didn't argue with me. She had obviously put two and two together, probably when he stuck her with that needle. She clawed the bracelet off her wrist and heaved it across the room. I pulled the last bit of tape free from her leg.

"Can you walk?" I asked her.

Rachel grabbed my face and quickly kissed my forehead. "I'm sorry I didn't believe you," she said.

"It's okay. But we really need to go." The three of us made a run for the door.

As we hit the hallway I could see Jake better with the office door open. Kory and I immediately grabbed him and tried pulling him up. I stumbled under his weight as the pain in my leg was now apparent.

"Hold on," Rachel said. She touched the top of Jake's head with her trembling hand. His body rose, still dead weight, still unconscious, until his feet were hovering only inches from the floor. We started down the hall with Jake's body following behind us.

A powerful blast of cold air filled the small hallway sending the three of us and Jake into the wall. Rachel lost focus and Jake crumpled to the floor. As we got back on our feet I saw the source of energy. Aiden stood in front of the Meeting room. He smiled at me as he backed slowly into the room, motioning for us to follow.

The three of us crept to the Meeting room entrance with Rachel in lead, although she was still wobbly from the drugs and blast of energy. Before I could grab her, Rachel was sucked into the room in a blink of an eye. The force sent her into the wall behind Aiden just barely missing the stained-glass windows. Kory and I immediately advanced into the room. Without saying a word, I knew my sister had the same thought. We needed to expel the demon and kill it.

The candles on the table lit up, illuminating Aiden's face. He turned, and his grin widened. His eyes had entirely turned black now. He raised his hands as if to hit us with another blast of energy, but Kory and I beat him to it. I felt the energy grow in the pit of my stomach and branch out to the tips of my fingers and toes. Heat enveloped me. Not like the heat blast Rachel had used on us before, but a great enormous power.

When the power escaped, it burst through my hands like red lightening. Kory focused her energy at the same time, rooting Aiden to the floor unable to move. He threw his head backward. As the energy continued to ignite his body, we watched in awe as his head swiveled even further backwards and with a crack it landed on the floor. Neither Kory nor I stopped the outpouring of energy as we watched a dark mass pull itself out of what had been Aiden's neck. When fully formed the black mass allowed its host body to drop. We raised our arms simultaneously transferring the energy from Aiden's fallen body to the demon. The demon groaned and twisted as it tried to manifest itself into its original form. Instinctively, I knew its original shape would be harder to kill.

"Ava!" Kory screamed, and I turned to see a black tentacle from the demon lash out and catch her in the face knocking her to the back of the room over the pews. When I turned to face the demon, it was too late. The tentacle whipped out at my shoulder. As it knocked me into the wall, I felt my shoulder crunch as pain raced through my body. I stood up, refusing to allow the increasing dizziness and pain to hold me back. This demon had to be stopped. It could not use Aiden's body anymore, but it would find another.

I rubbed at my shoulder and noticed the thick black goo I'd seen in the office fireplace. This same demon once inhabited the body of Lyle Carey, the founder of the Order. When Lyle became too old, the demon possessed his young student, Aiden. And I would bet anything, Jake was the demon's next host. I couldn't let it get to Jake's body in the hallway. Before I could position myself again, a pair of arms tackled me onto the floor.

"What's up, A?" Dillon hissed into my ear. I managed to turn over and face him. With his full weight on me, I was pinned to the floor. "I can't believe you girls were keeping this power from me. But, Elhath is making it right. Now with Aiden and Jake gone, I'm going to lead the Order with Kory by my side." He snarled his lip up at me.

"You killed Pastor Simms, didn't you?" I screamed up at him as I tried to break free from his grip on my wrists.

He shrugged. "Aiden said great power means great sacrifice."

"Yes, I guess it does." I pulled all the energy into myself and with a silent prayer, let it go. The enormous burst set Dillon on fire. His clothes went up in flames as he screamed and toppled backwards off me. I scurried away from him as he rolled on the Meeting room floor, but it was no use. Within seconds, Dillon was dead.

The demon writhed in the corner of the room, already partially formed. I couldn't see Kory from where I stood, but I pulled the energy and strength back through me. I tried to raise my arms, but the pain in my shoulder was too great. I prayed. I could not defeat this thing alone and if it got out, it would pull more souls into Hell using the Order of Greatness as its front.

I raised my left arm and the hot energy shocked through my palm. It hit the demon causing it to groan louder. The palm of my right hand began to burn with energy, but I still couldn't raise it to direct it at the demon.

A strong hand grabbed my wrist and I realized it was Calder. "Keep going," he shouted over the demon's wailing. He placed his other hand on my shoulder and squeezed. I almost fell to my knees from the excruciating pain, but Calder steadied me, and he pushed my shoulder back into the socket.

Two other streams of energy penetrated from the corner of the room. Rachel, finally on her feet, stood closer to the demon - her face streaked in tears and blood - she was fiercely battling the demon with every bit of energy she could summon. The demon tried to lash out at her but missed just as two more energy beams came from the back of the room. Kory walked up the center aisle, blood dripping down her face from her apparent head wound.

The demon's groans became louder and turned into a high-pitched scream. My ears pounded, but I refused to give in. My body burned with power, but we couldn't stop – not yet – although I wasn't sure how much longer any of us could continue.

The Meeting room began to shake as plaster fell from the ceiling. Suddenly, Calder lurched forward, causing me to drop my beam of energy. Roger wrestled with Calder on the floor in front of the stage. Roger's face was a twisted horror full of blood and tissue.

"Ava! Focus!" Rachel yelled over the screams.

I pulled the energy beam back to the demon and focused on it as Roger and Calder moved in and out of my peripheral vision. Calder had the man on the ground as he stood up and walked over to the Ogham stone tower. Roger laid on the floor groaning miserably. Finally, I found enough courage to look at Calder, in time to see the ancient being bring the pointed end of the stone tower down onto Roger's head, smashing it.

"Throw the dagger now!" Calder commanded, and I dropped the energy from my right arm as I pulled the dagger from Jake's belt and aimed it at Elhath. I threw it as hard as I could. The knife landed in the center of the black mass as the demon's high-pitched wails grew. I resumed the energy stream from my burning right arm. My body begged me to stop and rest, but I pushed on.

From down on his knees, Calder produced the last of Iris' blue stones and smiled wistfully at it as the stone continued to pulsate with energy. With a mighty clap, he smashed the quartz between his hands. Immediately, a large glowing hand appeared before the demon. It grabbed the demon around the body and squeezed as the demon screamed louder.

In a flash of bright light, the demon burst in all directions. Pieces of black slimy meat fell everywhere. As soon as it hit the ground, it shriveled and turned to ash. The energy beams stopped, and I fell to my knees.

The hand vanished as I closed my eyes and laid down on the stone floor, my head woozy from the loss of blood from my leg. I felt someone touch my cheek and I opened my eyes once more to see the young Iris from my vision leaning over me so close that I could smell the scent of flowers from her hair.

"Well done, my Ava Grace. It's time to rest now."

~ ~ ~

When I opened my eyes, I lay on a gurney in an ambulance with an oxygen mask over my face. Rachel sat beside me, holding my hand.

She leaned down and kissed my forehead when she saw I was awake. "Hey, pretty girl, you're awake. The paramedics stopped the bleeding from your leg. They said you're going to be fine." Then she whispered, "The demon is gone and won't possess anyone anymore." A sad look crossed over her face.

I removed the mask. "Where are Kory and Jake?" I asked, my voice sounded dry and unfamiliar.

"The paramedics had to bandage Kory's head. She's fine though, don't worry. I was just with her. Head wounds typically bleed more. I think they are going to transport her and Jake in another ambulance for observation. Jake's head wound is more severe. Aiden meant to kill him, so it's a miracle he's still alive."

I squeezed her hand. "I'm sorry it was Aiden. I know you loved him."

Rachel nodded and touched my hand to her face. "The thing is I didn't know it was him and now I think he was possessed the whole time I knew him. Then he blinded us from seeing who he really was with the bracelets. I got too close. I can never make that mistake again. When I saw him choking you, I wanted to stop him, but he compelled me to leave. I'm sorry, Ava. You and Kory are my world now. I promise you." She kissed my forehead again as the paramedics shut the door to the ambulance.

"Where's Calder and the dagger?"

"He had to return. He said if it wasn't for us standing strong and believing we could do it, the demon would've won. The dagger was destroyed along with the demon and-"

"But what about the hand?" I asked, as a paramedic guided the mask over my mouth again.

Rachel waited until the paramedic returned to his machines before answering quietly. "*That* was the hand of God Himself. Very rarely do you see Him move like that, but Calder assured me that He is always moving."

CHAPTER THIRTY-THREE

Two Months Later*

Standing in the kitchen in the house in Locklyn, I poured my first cup of coffee. It was a beautiful Saturday morning and the sunlight coming through the window lit up the whole room. I made my way to the front porch to sit in my favorite rocker. Kory Ann was still asleep in her little room and Mom was in the shower.

As I rocked, my foot touched the wooden porch slightly and I silently thanked God for the last two months. Mom and I were finally forming that bond I'd always yearned for, so I stopped calling her Rachel and started calling her Mom - to her face. Sometimes she seemed a bit sad and I wondered if she missed having a man in her life. That was until she met David. David managed the bookstore in town and they'd been going out for a couple of weeks now. It was too soon to tell, but he was dating a Brewer woman, so he was smitten.

Kory jumped back into her life as soon as her feet touched North Carolina soil, hanging out with her friends, going shopping, and going on dates. She'd mourned Dillon's death, of course, but understood that Aiden and the Order had tempted him, and he'd given in. He'd even gone so far as to kill Pastor Simms to prove his worth. Kory was going to be just fine.

The police in Locklyn had questioned me and Jake and we'd given them the planner, but Dillon had left behind fingerprints. Apparently, he'd come in Roger's place that morning. Without the Order to cover up the murder, all evidence pointed to Dillon.

As for me, Jake called and texted almost every day. After the destruction of the demon and Aiden's disappearance, the Order fell apart. The authorities treated the Order of Greatness as a crime organization led by Aiden. Carey House stood empty. Jake worked part-time while attending classes and scheduled a trip to North Carolina next month to visit me. I was excited about the idea of Jake and me. I didn't know if it would work since we lived in different states but seeing how hard it was for an Elemental to have a real relationship, I wanted to try.

I'd finally had the chance to tell Freya our incredible story, although I'm not sure she believed everything. She seemed to think Aiden being a mobster buying up the town was a much better fit. It didn't matter. We knew the truth.

I finished my coffee and then drove Iris' car, which was now mine, to the beach. The beach was a bit more populated this morning than I would have liked, but that was okay. I spread a towel on the sand and pulled my cover up off. As I soaked in the warmth from the sun's rays, I felt someone sit down next to me.

I opened my eyes to see Calder's sun kissed body beside mine. The other beach goers didn't seem to notice that the young man probably just walked out from the ocean, or the fact that the shadow hovering over us resembled large wings. Calder leaned over and nudged me, a playful smile on his lips.

Defeating demons for God may be my new normal and having a relationship with a human man may be something I would have to strive for as an Elemental, but something told me I would always have Calder by my side. Even without the blue stones.

THE END

ABOUT THE AUTHOR

Melissa Plantz is the author of the spiritual warfare devotional series, TAKE THE REALM; and the novels, FIRE AND GRACE and THE MULADACH (releasing Summer 2020). She is also the Founder of FIRE and GRACE Publishing, LLC (FireandGracePublishing.com) with the mission to equip today's Christians for spiritual warfare through the power of storytelling.

She currently lives in West Virginia with her husband and two youngest children, although not far from her adult children and two grandchildren. She dreams of moving permanently to a beach off the coast of North Carolina.

Connect with Melissa at :

AuthorMelissaPlantz@fireandgracepublishing.com

www.ingramcontent.com/pod-product-compliance
Lightning Source LLC
Chambersburg PA
CBHW022134240626
47153CB00007B/2366